Of Water and Fire

Claire Davon

Cover Design: Maroli Design Services

Claire Davon
P.O. Box 731
Van Nuys, CA 91408

Publishing History
Of Water and Fire
First Digital Publication: December, 2018
Second Digital Publication: April, 2019
First Print Publication: April, 2019
Siren's Crush
First Digital Publication: June, 2017
Second Digital Publication: April, 2019
First Print Publication: April, 2019
Rising Melody
First Digital Publication: November, 2016
Second Digital Publication: April, 2019
First Print Publication: April, 2019

ISBN: 978-1-946621-09-2

Introduction

This book compiles two stories centered around the same characters and an unrelated siren story. The first story, *Of Water and Fire* was actually the second written about the couple. Its events take place after the events of the second story *Siren's Crush. Rising Melody*, the third story, involves a siren who wishes to fly and while it takes place in the same world as the first two stories, is not part of their adventure.

I hope that everyone who likes a good tale (tail?) of sirens or mermaids enjoys this collection.

Happy reading!

Table of Contents

Of Water and Fire

Foreword

Of Water and Fire was included in a collection of mermaid and siren stories called *Voices of the Deep*. It was a limited term release and the collection was taken offline as of March 19, 2019. I was thrilled with the opportunity to include this novella as part of that collection. Gabe and Emilia's tale had just started at the time of *Siren's Crush* and the opportunity to delve further into their love story was too delicious to resist.

Chapter 1

"You'd be prettier with more makeup on."

Emilia looked over at the speaker, trying not to show her surprise at the comment. A tall man in his early twenties stood in the common area. Emilia took a step back to put distance between herself and the looming stranger. Her senses buzzed, letting her know she wasn't looking at a mortal.

"Do I know you?" Emilia tried to keep her voice calm, although his words coupled with the half sneer expression on his face made bile rise in her throat.

He leaned in and Emilia glanced around. People were coming and going from classes, buzzing from one place to the next like bees in a busy hive. Gabe, the guy she had been seeing for a little over a month, wasn't in class today.

A flash from his phone told Emilia that the stranger had taken a picture of her. She stared at the offending device and then back to the man. "Pictures come out better when people have makeup on. Everyone says they like the natural look but they don't." His smirk faded, replaced by a cocky grin. "I'm Rector Lyson. Maybe you've heard of me?"

She shook her head. Rector was handsome in a classical sense, with an expensive haircut framing his perfect features and a muscled, well-built body, but there was an aura about him that made her want to back away. She wished Gabe were here.

Or not. She was a siren. She could handle one boy.

"Sorry, I haven't."

"Let me show you what I mean." He gestured for her to step closer but Emilia remained where she was.

"No, thanks. I don't care what I look like in your photo. Please delete it. I don't like having my picture taken."

Fury swam over his features that was at odds with her simple request. Emilia glanced around, wondering if she was going to have a problem.

"Your loss. I can make you famous. I'm a travel blogger. I go to campuses and check out the culture. I've got a bunch of followers on social media." He said this as though he didn't know how many supporters he had but Emilia bet he knew down to the last person.

"I don't want to be famous."

Rector's smile widened and there was something predatory about the grin. His face was unnaturally handsome in the way of actors…or gods. There was no question that he was something other than human. Of course he was. With a face that perfect he had to be from one of the pantheons.

"Nonsense. Everyone does."

"Not me. Please delete my picture."

He made no move toward the phone.

"I'm doing a piece on the University of Hawaii. What kid doesn't dream of coming here. I want to feature some of the local students. You would be great, if you just shaded your eyes a bit more, and had more color in your cheeks."

Every inch told her to wrestle the phone from his grasp to get rid of the picture, even though she was trying to stay calm. She kept her social media profile to a minimum and didn't allow friends to tag her. Given who she was, it was best not to draw attention to herself.

"There are dozens of gorgeous women on campus but I'm not one of them. I asked you to please delete my picture. I don't want it in your blog."

She thought for a moment he was going to refuse but then with an exaggerated sigh Rector thumbed through the phone and pressed a button. She would have no way of knowing if he actually deleted the thing, but that was about as good as she was going to get.

"Too bad. I guess I have to up my game to get you to agree," he said and winked at her. "After all, we mythical types have to stick together."

She kept her face in a bland expression although her roiling stomach was now doing cartwheels.

"We…what?"

He leaned in. Emilia steeled her face to show no fear. If questioned she couldn't have said what it was about Rector that made her dislike him on sight.

"I know what you are. A siren."

Emilia tried not to react. Her heart pounded with a fierce thump and she thought she was going to pass out.

"Don't worry, though," he said with that same predatory smile. "There's nothing to fear. I've got secrets of my own. I'm Lyssa's great-grandson. I want to hear you sing."

⁂

Gabe woke up to the feel of the earth rumbling under his feet.

It took him a moment to realize that it was just the transition from sleep to waking and the earth wasn't actually moving. He could feel the lingering after effects of the dream in the way he wanted to roll off the bed and onto the floor.

He waited a moment and when nothing else happened, eased his legs down. The room stayed steady and he let out his breath. He felt a rumble deep in his belly that had little to do with hunger. Glancing at the clock told him was too early to text Emilia. She would still be sleeping.

Scratching himself, he went into the tiny kitchen of his single apartment and scrounged for something to eat. Nothing leaped into view so he sighed and closed the refrigerator door.

He listened to the ground, disturbed by what he had felt before. When he felt no further disturbances, Gabe breathed out a sigh of relief. Sending a word of thanks to Pele, he made his way to the shower.

Afterward Gabe headed for campus. Much as he wanted to talk to Emilia their relationship was too new to text her for no particularly good reason. He hoped that would change soon but he wasn't pushing it. They were together, and that was the only thing that mattered.

Gabe went to the library and pulled out his tablet to study for his exam while things were quiet. The rumbling of the volcano troubled him but as he heard nothing further he had to be content with that. His blood was so diluted that he was not immortal or much of a demi-god. There were many like him in the world.

He felt a presence ping on his senses that told him there was another like him around. He craned his neck, hoping to see Emilia, but saw nothing besides the stacks of books and students with their heads bent, intent on their assignments.

The thought of Emilia made him smile. They'd only been dating for a little while but he knew from the moment he met her that she was different than any other woman he'd ever known. She was a siren, and she was Emilia. They understood one another in ways that a human could never do.

He felt that ping again that told him someone other than a human was nearby.

"Hi there," a voice said and Gabe's radar pinged again. He turned his head and looked to see a man about his age leaning over the table, looking at him.

"Hi," Gabe said and rose. He was taller but the other guy was more handsome, even to Gabe's masculine eye. He had the look of a person who retained the ability to shape their looks to whatever they wanted, as gods did. That told him that the stranger had far more god blood than Gabe did.

"I'm Rector Lyson. Lyssa's great-grandson."

Boom. Right off the bat. Lyssa. Gabe frowned for a moment trying to recall who Lyssa was. Not part of the major pantheon. She was…

"Goddess of strife and discord," Rector supplied, an easy smile on his lips. His perfect features twitched, the corners of his mouth tugging up. He stuck out his hand. "You're Gabe, great whatever grandson of Hephaestus. I felt you when I got on campus, you and the other one. I wanted to introduce myself. I've got a blog, perhaps you've heard of me."

There was something about the aggressive smile that Gabe didn't like.

"Nice to meet you," Gabe said in a cool tone, holding Rector's hand a bit too tight. He didn't let go until Rector winced slightly. Then he released the other demi-god's hand and grinned without mirth.

"I already introduced myself to Emilia earlier. She's something. I want her in the blog. And I want to hear her sing."

Gabe took a step forward, wanting to slam his hands onto the table, or push the man. The sudden fury wasn't like him and he took a few breaths to calm himself.

"She's private. She doesn't sing, and I doubt she'd want to be in any blog. How did you meet…" Gabe paused and then mentally shrugged and continued "…my girlfriend?" If they hadn't quite established that yet then Rector didn't need to know that particular truth.

"I took her picture. I felt her when I came on campus. A siren, nice. You're a lucky guy."

Rector's handsome face went ugly for a moment and Gabe tensed, his hands curling into fists. As the great-grandson of the goddess of rage and frenzy, or whatever it was, he had to have abilities along those lines. Gabe would have to read up on the woman.

Haleakalā rumbled, a minute tremor, but Gabe felt it low in his belly. They were far enough away that the rumble wasn't noticeable to someone not sensitive, although he was sure the meters tracking the volcano picked it up.

"I am fortunate," he agreed. "We both are. Fair warning, Rector. She's mine."

There were other students around but nobody was paying them any attention, except to give Rector admiring looks. Gabe faded next to the demi-god's shining attractiveness. He normally wouldn't care but right now he wanted to rearrange that too-perfect face.

"Is that right? I know something about sirens and they're not the settling down kind. I can take all the time I need on this blog. I'll wear her down until she changes her mind. Be warned. I'm coming after her."

"You'll have to go through me."

Rector straightened and smiled, his perfect white teeth gleaming. "I have no problem with that."

Haleakalā rumbled on a subsonic level, and Gabe saw Rector twitch but he did nothing further. Gabe could feel the volcano as minute tremors under his skin but it seemed the other man did not. Interesting.

"Touch her and you'll be sorry."

"Threats will get you nowhere. All I need is a little bit of time to convince her. If not, there are always other ways. I'd say it was good to meet a fellow godling, but I'd be lying. See you soon."

With that Rector smiled, saluted and walked off. Gabe wanted to ram his fist into the table but settled for sitting down and heading for the search engines.

Time to learn more about Lyssa.

&

"That's the same thing he said to you?" Emilia tried to identify the expression on Gabe's face. Anger. Worry. Fear.

"He said he was the great-grandson of Lyssa, the goddess of rage and frenzy. She's a minor goddess. I looked her up."

She tapped her phone. "I looked him up too and checked his blog. It's the usual blogger stuff. There's more on Lyssa. I had no idea who she was. It isn't just rage and frenzy. She also is supposed to cause rabies in animals. Like her great-grandson," Emilia said, and was gratified when Gabe gave a grunt of amusement.

They were sitting at Lahaina Fish Co, looking out over the water as the sun began its descent below the horizon. Maybe later when the sun went down she would take a dip in the ocean. If she went under water fast she could change and spend time with the marine life without detection. It was a risk but she hated being out of the ocean for too long. She wished she had a pool like her folks did, for those times when it was too risky to be seen in the waves.

"He probably has rabies," Gabe grumbled, and Emilia grinned at his response. As much as Rector's bold advance had unnerved her, seeing Gabe made it all better. She didn't care about Rector's passes, what concerned her more was that he knew who she was. What she was.

"How does he know about me?" She glanced at Gabe, who was summoning the waiter to bring a dessert menu.

Gabe leaned forward and pressed a kiss against her cheek. "He's a demi-god. I felt him too. It's the same way I knew there was something different about you even before I knew what you were. He sensed the otherness in you. I want him to leave you alone. He's a punk and that blog of his is stupid fluff. Lots of pictures of himself eating and hot girls. Some blogger. I don't like the way he told me he was going to try to get you. You're my girl, not his."

That was Gabe for you, big and solid like a rock.

"I didn't lead him on. I didn't like him, Gabe. I made him delete the picture. There was something unnerving about him. Maybe it's the goddess he's descended from."

Gabe shrugged. "Yeah, could be. She's a nasty piece of work. Normally I don't hold a person's origins against them but I'm making an exception for him. I'll rearrange that perfect face if you want."

She laid her hand over his. Gabe laced their fingers together and squeezed.

"No need for violence. I am not interested in him."

"He thinks he's better than me because he has more god cred than I do."

She shook her head. "I don't care about that. I wouldn't want him if he were full god."

"He wants you because you're a siren. That's what he said. Something about singing for him."

Emilia closed her eyes for a moment. "He doesn't know what he's asking. Our song is dangerous. I won't sing for him. Our songs are precious to us and not shared with strangers."

For a moment she wondered if he was going to ask for her song. Then Gabe nodded and stroked her hand.

"It's your choice, Emy. It's always your choice."

She thought she felt a presence in her mind, like an octopus only it was a man who was much more than a man. Then it was gone but it left a ripple in her mind like ocean waves. She reached out but the presence eluded her. It felt like Kanaloa, the sea god, but he had never approached Emilia before. She dismissed it, for the moment.

"Rector won't get a song out of me."

"Good."

Chapter 2

Gabe lay in his bed and listened to Haleakalā rumble, too low for anyone but him and any earth powers around to hear. The feeling rolled through him and continued until he rose.

His neck hairs prickled and Gabe stopped in the middle of the room. His tiny studio was in darkness with a hint of early morning light coming through the window.

Nothing seemed disturbed. Not his blinds, not the floor, not his neighbors who surely would have been woken if the volcano was stirring to life. He felt molten earth reaching toward the volcano.

He had a glimpse of a woman with dark hair and a crown of red flowers around her head. Her body was clad in a flowing red robe and the rock seemed to flow as though it was part of her clothing. She looked at him for a long moment, her face unreadable. Her hair streamed out from her body like it was touched by wind. She dipped her hand through the burning, flowing rock, and it came away unhurt.

Pele, he thought, and she nodded but said nothing. Then the goddess' spirit flowed away, disappearing into the lava. Sweat broke out on his skin.

Haleakalā rumbled.

"I'd like to hear you sing."

Rector's voice cut into her reverie. When she didn't respond, he tapped her on the shoulder. Emilia shuddered but didn't look his direction.

"Go away, Rector."

"Don't be rude. I said I'd like to hear you sing. It's what you folks do, after all."

The crush of college students was thick around them. Emilia was conscious of a few curious looks.

The blogger's arrival had created a sensation on the Maui campus. Emilia may never have heard of him but that wasn't true of others. His blog had thousands of followers, enough to make him a minor celebrity.

She narrowed her eyes at Rector and folded the laptop she'd been on in case she had to make a quick escape.

"I don't sing," she said in a flat tone. "Leave me alone. You're bothering me. I told you I had a boyfriend."

He smiled but there was nothing pleased in that smile.

"Imagine my surprise when I find a siren here neatly tucked away in the school, behaving just like a human. You're somewhat pretty as well, although no take on goddesses, of course."

She raised her eyebrows at this.

"Rector, insulting me won't help you achieve your goal. I don't sing for strangers. I don't allow bloggers to post my picture and I don't like arrogant gods."

His laugh was harsh and made a few people stop. One or two women gave her a concerned look but she waved them off.

"That's a lie, siren. Your so-called boyfriend is like me, but several generations more diluted. I'm more powerful than he is. You should be grateful I'm showing you interest. I'm much higher on the pantheon than he is."

"I don't care about that. Even if Gabe weren't a factor, I wouldn't be interested."

"So you say. I'll get what I want in the end." Before she could stop him, he raised his camera and took another picture. Emilia opened her mouth and then shut it. He leaned in and she could smell an odd scent, like wildlife. Emilia wanted to pull back but also didn't want to show fear.

"You will sing for me. My dad says there's nothing like it on earth. Give me what I want and I'll go away."

She shook her head. "You don't know what you're asking."

He shrugged. "My dad heard you guys and said nothing bad happened to him. He said you were like angels. I want to hear it for myself."

His words were casual but there was an odd desperation in his eyes, like this was far more important than he was letting on.

"I said no, Rector. Now you're just being annoying. Didn't your mother ever tell you to take no for an answer?"

He laughed and the sound had a tint of malice to it. "My mom? She's Lyssa's granddaughter. What do you think?"

"I think she spoiled you too much so you don't know how to take no for an answer. And no is my only response."

For a moment Rector looked murderous and Emilia felt a ping of alarm. Many emotions clashed over his face before settling on rage. Then it was gone.

"We'll see, siren. I always get what I want in the end."

"I don't know why you keep persisting. Stop bugging me to do something I'm not going to do."

She spun on her heel, trying to get away before the shaking began.

"You'll give me what I want. Mark my words."

"Not a chance."

His mocking laugh floated after her, but he didn't pursue.

❧ ☙

Emilia felt hands around her eyes, coupled with the scent of Gabe. He always smelled faintly of fire. It was only when she was close to him that she sensed the combination of charred wood and smoke that was somehow not unpleasant.

"Surprise," he said in a husky tone.

She turned to him and slid her arms around him. He looked down at her and brushed her hair back off her cheek.

"Surprise? I just saw you," she said and tilted her head up to him. Gabe seemed to take the hint and skimmed a kiss over her lips. She sighed against him and closed her eyes. There had always been something reassuring about Gabe. With him she felt safe and never judged. Gabe always made her feel cherished—an asset to his life. Gabe gave her the self-assurance she had been lacking growing up.

He chuckled and kissed her again. They were in the common area of the school, the grassy lawn and benches a favorite spot for students to perch between classes.

"Surprise. I wasn't supposed to be done this early but the teacher was sick and they didn't get a sub in time, so I'm free. I know you don't have another class until three, so we have a few hours to ourselves. Want to get some lunch? I'm starved."

As though on cue his stomach growled. Emilia thought she heard a faint echo of a rumble of Haleakalā under her feet, but it was too indistinct to be sure. Gabe had said that he had very little god power, and there was no reason to think the volcano would be responding to him. It was probably just the natural movement of the earth in this part of the world.

"Lunch?" she asked, squeezing his fingers when he took her hand. She loved the feel of his warm palm against hers, even in the humid Maui day.

His shaggy brown hair was getting longer. On others it might look unkempt but there was nothing about Gabe that was wrong. She was aware that she was in like, and possibly, could love Gabe.

Her life as a human was fragile and any incorrect move could jeopardize that peace. Her mother told her that it was unlikely humans would believe they saw a siren, or more likely a mermaid, in these waters, but she also cautioned Emilia to be careful. In this day and age the possibility of being watched, or recorded, lurked in her mind. It would only take one drone to capture their blue and green tails, their fins and their gills and blast it on social media for their secret to be exposed. Most would think it was photoshopped or edited, but not everyone.

They went to a local taco place that overlooked the water, with a spectacular view of the surf pounding against the shore. Here the waves were rough, the landscape unsuitable for tanners or swimmers. For anyone except someone like her.

After they had ordered, Gabe studied her face. "Has that creep Rector left you alone?"

She slid her hand over his, loving the warm feel of his skin, wanting more of him, and more. There was something so natural about being with Gabe, like he was, and had always been, part of her family.

"Not really. The ladies on campus love him and trail him around like little ducklings. He keeps taking my picture, although I keep telling him I won't be in his blog. He wants me to sing for him."

Gabe's eyebrows raised. "No way. I know what that means to you. You're not considering it, are you? He's a handsome guy. I've heard the other students talk about him. I hear he is quite charming."

"It's wasted on me," she said and nudged his foot under the table. "There's only room in my life for one demi-god and that position is taken. I don't know him and I don't care to. Singing is out of the question."

Gabe smiled but there was something edgy about the look.

"Don't you believe me?"

Emilia tried not to let him see how badly that disbelief stung but knew she failed when he raked a hand through his hair and gave her a rueful glance.

"It's not you I'm worried about. I don't want to lose you, Emy. You're…precious to me."

For a heart stopping moment she thought he was going to say he loved her. Every cell waited for that moment. But Gabe said nothing further. Emilia gave him a quick look and he returned her stare without expression.

Her mother always instilled in Emilia a sense of the responsibility of being a siren. They may not be favored by the gods but they still had a great deal of power. It was one of the many reasons she did not sing. To do so would be to risk everything. She had to avoid the too-confident Rector who could expose everything she held dear with one careless post on his blog.

She smiled at Gabe, suppressing her disappointment when he said nothing else, and picked up her menu.

"I'm starved," she said.

❧ ☙

"When can I hear you sing?"

Emilia jumped at the sound of Rector's voice. She had been absorbed in her tablet, repeating the lesson from her Civics class to herself in preparation for a test the following day. Not long until she got out of school.

"You can't," she replied, sliding her hands into the straps of her backpack and readying to slide it off if necessary. "For the last time, leave it alone."

"Aw c'mon," Rector said. "My dad did everything he could trying to find a way to hear it again but the sirens refused. I want to hear what all the fuss is about. You will sing for me."

She dug her hands deeper into her pack straps, shrugging it forward until it fell off her shoulders. Then she pulled it off one shoulder and slung it around one arm, letting it fall loose.

"No. I don't hand out melodies to just anyone." She looked around at the swaying palm trees as they moved in the gentle breeze of the school courtyard. "It's dangerous."

It had recently rained in a typical afternoon shower and the paths were wet. Rector looked unruffled but Emilia was a bit damp, her hair clinging to her neck in moist strands. Normally she didn't care, but next to this perfect god she felt at a disadvantage. Any weakness in front of Rector was risky.

Rector gave a harsh grunt. "Dangerous? Only if you're a mortal, or a weak god like your so-called boyfriend. One song. I'll take you to dinner and then we can go down to the beach and you can sing. That's all I want."

Emilia looked at Rector, seeing the too-handsome face. There was something abnormal about his extreme attractiveness, like he had been photoshopped into perfection.

"I don't want to go to dinner with you."

He grabbed her left hand and Emilia resisted an urge to flinch and pull away. She readied the pack to swing at him.

"I don't see a ring on that finger. Your boyfriend hasn't made you any promises, and even if he did, so what? People come and go all the time. You're not married, or engaged, so you can go to dinner with me. One date. Dinner and singing."

Emilia wanted to run from him but you didn't flee from bullies. Instead she straightened and looked him right in the eye. Rector grinned, tossing his hair back from his head, and seemed confident of his ability to lure her into his wishes.

"No," she said.

"What?" He looked stunned, although she couldn't imagine why.

"No. I don't want to go to dinner with you. I don't want to sing for you. I don't want anything to do with you, Rector." She thrust her chin up. "I'm not going to go out with you. Besides the fact that Gabe wouldn't like it, I wouldn't like it."

"He controls everything you do?" Rector said in a challenging tone, his posture turning from pleading to aggressive. He widened his stance, pushing his lower body forward. Emilia took a step back.

"No, he does not." She suspected that Rector might be the gaslighting/controlling type, judging on how unwilling he was to take no for an answer. She bet other women had given in to him, ones seduced by the perfection of his visage.

"Then you can go out with me."

"I could, but I don't want to. I am not averse to going out with friends." Emilia paused, knowing the next words were unwise, but unable to stop herself. "We're not friends, Rector. You barged into my life and have been demanding I do something I don't want to do for days now. I keep saying no but you don't respect it. I'm not going out with you. I'm not going to sing for you. Get over your bad self, demi-god, because it isn't going to happen. Leave me alone."

She spun on her heel and left. The last image she saw was of a furious looking Rector staring after her.

❧ ❧

"Let's go for a boat ride."

Emilia gave Gabe a questioning look.

"Like tourists? Go around the island and see the sights? Why would we do that?"

Gabe rolled his eyes in a broad gesture that told her he was having fun with her.

"No, silly siren. We should rent a speedboat and go along the coast, then into deeper water so you can, you know, play with the dolphins in your other form."

Emilia's face pulled down in a frown and Gabe's expectant look changed to one of alarm.

"What is it, Emy? I thought you'd be happy at the idea. I know how much the water means to you."

"It does," she said and slid her hand into his. "I'd love to. I just worry about exposure."

He pulled her to him and kissed her forehead. "We'll be careful. I know you want to swim with the dolphins. Are you worried about sharks? I can bring shark repellent."

Emilia laughed. "Sharks are as much fun as dolphins or sea lions. You know dolphins are predators, right? They eat fish and the things they do to get their meals are often quite brutal. I'm not worried about sharks. It's the human, or god types, that concern me."

"You've got nothing to be concerned about. That jerk won't know we're going. I'll make sure of it."

Despite her trepidation the lure of the ocean was too great to resist. "Then I'm in. When did you have in mind?"

His grin, and the way he ducked his head, was so endearing she couldn't resist brushing the stray lock of hair back. Gabe took her hand and pressed a kiss into the center of her palm.

"This weekend. I'll make the arrangements. I wish I could see all that with you. I'll learn to SCUBA so I can go down too. Would you like that?"

For a moment Emilia hesitated. The only other person she'd ever shared her underwater adventures with was her mother.

"I'd like that," she said and he breathed out. "I usually go alone and I go pretty far down," she warned, combing her hand through his hair.

"I won't cramp your style," he said with a grumble.

"How does that work with a fire god?"

He grinned. "We don't steam the place up if that's what you mean. I'm not allergic to water, or anything like that. I just run hotter than other people. Sometimes I can sense volcanos. Like Haleakalā."

"Really?"

His eyes searched hers for long moments before he responded. "It feels me and I feel it. It's alive but not in the same way you and I are. It's more…elemental than that. It seems to…I dunno…want something from me. I can't figure it out," he paused and gulped, his throat working. "I sensed Pele, too."

Emilia said nothing for a moment and then smiled, leaning in to kiss him.

"I thought I felt Kanaloa recently as well. It's interesting. All this time you've been saying that you barely have any god blood and yet here you are talking to volcanos. I think Hephaestus runs deeper in you than you know."

He let out a relieved breath. "You don't mind? I haven't been sure how to tell you."

Emilia gave Gabe another kiss.

"I don't mind. You and I have a lot to learn about each other. Should I be worried about Pele? I hear she's a very jealous goddess."

His look of relief was so evident that she had to suppress a smile.

"I don't think so, although who can tell with gods? What about you and Kanaloa?"

"Nope. You are full of surprises, Gabe, and I like it."

"Good." He pointed to the water and gathered her close. "I'll let you know about the boat ride."

She nodded. "I wouldn't miss it for the world."

Chapter 3

"There's a choir in the school."

Emilia let out an audible groan and turned to face her nemesis. Rector stood there with a big grin on his face, his camera at the ready while striking a model-like pose.

"Rector, how many times do I have to tell you I am not going to sing."

He moved closer so she backed up a step.

"You can say it a million times and I won't care. I'm going to get what I want, so you might as well do it so I'll leave you alone."

Visions of what the great-grandson of the goddess of frenzy could do dashed through Emilia and she shuddered. Her powers were better suited on the water where she had more strength and control. If she tried to use them on land she was weaker and almost helpless.

"No thanks, Rector, I am not interested."

"Leave my girlfriend alone."

Gabe's voice came out of nowhere. She glanced over at her angry looking boyfriend and then back at Rector. The other man was still in an easy posture but his body lines had gone tense.

"I don't see a ring. You're not married."

"She's my girl."

Rector cocked an eyebrow at Emilia. "Does he speak for you? I thought all you modern women took care of yourself. Are you going to hide behind him and let him do your fighting?"

Gabe's fists came up and Emilia saw that his face was reddening. "I'm happy to fight, you son of a bitch."

Rector put his pack down and raised his own hands. "That's no way to talk about my mother, you half bit godling. I'm much more powerful than you are, asshole!"

Emilia stepped between the men. She would be thrilled to see Rector pummeled but that could get Gabe expelled from school for fighting.

"It's okay, Gabe," she said, putting her hand on his arm. Gabe glanced down but then looked back at Rector, still in a fighting stance. Any moment now one of the men was going to go for the other. She looked around and a few students were eyeing them with curiosity. Rector looked amused by the whole episode.

She lowered her gaze, trying to hide her unease. It would do no good to fan the flames of this already volatile situation, much as she wanted to. "He thinks if he tries hard enough he can get me to sing. It's this crazy obsession of his."

"Have you heard her? Has she sung for you?" Rector looked eager, his too handsome face somehow managing to look even more attractive. She wondered if it was her siren blood that made her immune from what would otherwise be hard to resist.

"If she ever chooses to sing for me it would be an honor to hear her. But siren songs are dangerous and Emilia knows the power of her melody."

Rector unclenched his hands and stepped back. Making a dismissive gesture, he looked over at the duo with contempt replacing the eagerness.

"You're scared, halfling. Scared that her song will lure you to your death. Didn't she tell you that Odysseus was just a guy scorned? He filled people's heads with nonsense about the sirens after they booted him from the island. That's what great grandma said and I believe her. Dad heard them and he didn't go crazy. You're right to be scared, Gabriel. Your girlfriend needs a real god."

For a moment she wanted to give Rector an earful of siren song. She even opened her mouth and began to hum before catching Gabe's alarmed face and subsided.

"Emilia, don't."

Rector looked eager but when Emilia didn't continue, his face fell. For a moment, rage flooded his expression distorting it in a grotesque mask of fury. In that moment she had no trouble understanding his heritage. Her breathing caught and her heart skipped a beat while sweat broke out on her forehead. All Rector did was stand there but in that moment he terrified her. He adjusted his pack while his face cleared and he smiled, though it didn't reach his eyes.

"You will regret crossing me. Nobody tells me no."

"We just did," Gabe said, putting his arm around Emilia.

"For now. I get what I want. Mark my words."

He left then, snapping pictures as he walked down the pathway. Within moments students surrounded him and Rector began talking to them in loud tones, his humor apparently restored.

"Maybe I should just give him a song to shut him up," she mused, looking to the small knot of people. Rector looked over at her and blew her a kiss before returning his attention to the others. Emilia shuddered. "If I did what he wanted then he would have nothing to say. It might be easier than fighting."

"No way," Gabe said, putting his other arm around her and hugging her. "Not unless you want to."

She shook her head. "I don't. He doesn't understand what he's asking. A siren's voice is a powerful weapon but he seems to think it's a play toy."

"Then you won't. You don't have to do anything you don't want to."

She shuddered, thinking of the fury in Rector's eyes and the absolute rage she saw in his body.

He wouldn't let it go. Deep down inside, she knew that.

❧ ☙

Emilia's eyes widened as she stared at the message sent to her email. With shaking fingers, she reached for her phone and sent Gabe a text and a forward.

Moments later her phone rang.

"I'm going to kill him," he said.

"That's what he wants," she replied and then scanned the message again. It was short but to the point. As a warning it was crude and not at all subtle but effective.

The post was about a "supernatural creature" sighting stating that sirens had been spotted in Maui. A blurry picture of a humanoid form with a tail accompanied the article, with a promise that "more would be revealed."

She had been foolish to think he would just walk away. She should have known better.

The other shoe, proverbially, had dropped.

"He can't do this," Gabe said, steel in his voice.

"He can and he did."

As though in confirmation her email chimed with another anonymous email. This time it was a picture of her with a tail neatly superimposed over her legs. She peered at the accompanying words.

"This is photoshopped but it doesn't matter. Sing for me or I'll call you a mermaid. I've got enough followers that if I ask them to repost my stuff they will. Soon you will be world famous as the mermaid lady. This is your fault. You should have given me what I wanted. You have a week to set up a plan to sing for me or this is my next blog. I've got the headline already. 'Rector goes to Maui and discovers a mermaid.'"

Emilia forwarded that email to Gabe as well.

"He's a dead man," Gabe said, rage shaking his voice. "He can't do this to you."

She had no doubt Rector would make good on his threat. Even if most people laughed at the idea of mermaids—or sirens—there would be some who believed it. For all she knew the government would get involved.

"He can and he did," she said, weariness crushing her. All she wanted to do was lay down and hide but she couldn't do that.

"I have to sing for him, Gabe. I don't have a choice."

"Yes, you do," he insisted and Emilia felt her temper flare.

"What option do I have, Gabe? What do you want me to do? Tell him no and have him tell the entire world who I am? Expose me, and worse, my mom and all the sirens? For all we know he could tell everyone about the island and then people will be hunting for it."

"That happens anyway. It's a risk in this modern world," Gabe said. "Besides, he's bluffing. He can't reveal you without exposing himself."

"He's a blogger, Gabe. He'll get all his fans to dox me. They will flood my inbox, maybe even send death threats, and he would be untouched."

She thought she felt the earth move minutely but it was gone before she could be sure.

"How can I help? I hate seeing you like this."

"I don't know, I honestly don't. Look, I have to go." She hung up abruptly and threw herself back onto her bed. She had no idea what she would do next.

❧ ☙

For two days Emilia had dodged his calls and wasn't where he was expecting her to be on campus. The little worm, Rector, also was nowhere to be found which was a very good thing because Gabe wouldn't have been able to stop himself from kicking his ass. His heart felt like it had been torn from his chest because she bolted at the first sign of trouble even after showing how much he cared.

"Why the long face?"

Gabe turned, knowing it wasn't Emilia, but hoping that she was with the speaker. She wasn't.

"Hi, Maleko," he said, holding out his hand to the man. Maleko was native to the area with dark hair and dusky skin; he looked like a throwback to the days when Hawaii had kings and queens.

"Aloha, Gabriel," Maleko said. As schoolmates and occasional drinking buddies, he knew Maleko, but not well. The other man met his gaze until Gabe dropped his eyes.

"Something on your mind, buddy?" Gabe asked.

Maleko pointed around the courtyard. "Where's Emilia?"

"Things are fine."

"The volcanos say otherwise. Pele is unhappy."

Gabe blinked. "That's crazy," he stammered.

"You know that is not true," Maleko said. "Come. Let's sit. You can tell me what is going on and why your woman isn't around."

"I'm not sure she's my woman anymore," he admitted and saying the words out loud made his heart stutter. Pain, low and strong, coursed through his body until he wanted to bend over from the hurt.

Maleko patted him on the shoulder and led Gabe to the courtyard where he sat heavily on a stone bench.

"Tell me where the siren has gone. The gods are unhappy about the arrogant godling who caused it."

"For the love of…" A swear exploded out of Gabe and a woman near him turned. He ducked his head and waved an apology.

Maleko tilted his eyes down, drawing Gabe's attention. Maleko's hand shifted, grey hide replacing skin and his fingers elongating. In a moment his hand went back to normal.

"What are you, some sort of dolphin?" Gabe asked, leaning over so that only Maleko could hear him.

"*Niuhi*," Maleko said. *Shark*, Gabe translated, and eyed his friend. "I also serve Pele. We have known you were here since you came to campus. Emilia is long known to the marine life on her island, and she is welcome. You were a *haole*, a wild card, but you have proven that you respect our traditions."

Gabe found himself telling Maleko everything, from Rector's early advances to his threat. Maleko listened without comment and then rose.

"Do not let Rector win in this. You must stop him, Gabe, or the wrath of the gods may be terrible."

A new voice cut into their conversation. "The wrath of the gods? Why would they be angry at Gabe? I'm the one Rector is after."

When she spoke, Gabe whirled. She held her breath, only letting it out when she saw the relief in his eyes.

"Hi," he said, shuffling his feet before glancing up at her, his hair partially covering his face. She thought her heart would stop from the sheer joy of seeing him.

"Hi," she returned and bit her lip.

They both started speaking at once, tripping over each other's sentences in a tangle before Emilia stopped talking and looked at him. She half smiled and put her hand on his arm.

Maleko gave them a searching glance from under his thick lashes. "You are right, Emilia. It is you Rector wants. He does not understand the power of a siren's song or our gods. Be careful. Aloha."

She watched him go, glad to see the man leave. When he was out of sight she met Gabe's eyes, seeing that they had never wavered from hers. There was a question in the downward curve of his lips and the creases in his brow.

"Gabe, I'm sorry. I got scared."

"I'm here for you, Emy. I would never let anything happen to you."

She lowered her gaze to the sidewalk and scuffed at the concrete with her sneaker. It took all the bravery she had, but Emilia met Gabe's eyes again. When she saw nothing but understanding and compassion she felt even more ashamed. Before she could lower her eyes again Gabe gripped her chin and stilled her movement.

"I mean it," he said. "Let Rector do his worst. You and I will deal with it together."

Emilia trembled at the memory of Rector's threat. Gabe slid his arms around her and pulled her close. She let him in gladly, his warm, almost hot, body a balm to her troubled mind.

"I know what you need," he said after they held each other for several moments. She raised her head and gave him a quizzical look.

"What's that?"

His smile was lopsided. He touched her cheek with a hand that was so gentle she wanted to cry. All the worries about Rector fled. It didn't matter in that moment what happened. She was where she belonged—with Gabe. Always with Gabe.

"You need to be in your other form. We still have that boat reserved."

"But...Rector…" She sputtered the words even as her body thrilled to the idea of being in the water.

"He gave you a few more days, remember? We should do it now before his deadline gets closer. We planned on the weekend but hell with that. Today works too. I know how miserable you are. The water is calling."

She could almost hear the voices of the sea life calling to her. Could picture her tail propelling her through the currents as she sang to the marine creatures around her and cavorted with them. Yes. *Yes.*

"Okay. Thank you, Gabe."

His smile was a touch melancholy, as though the grip of their brief separation hadn't yet left him. "Of course," was all he said.

❧ ❧

"How are you doing back there?"

Gabe's voice broke into her reverie. She admired his strong form as he manned the controls, every inch a proud sailor. He was a fire power and water was not his medium.

He had done this for her despite the fact that Pele gave up her power to the sea god Kanaloa out here.

"I'm doing great, Gabe. Thank you for this. I didn't know how badly I needed it until we got on the water."

His smile lit up her world.

"We should do this every weekend. Maybe I can get a boat of my own."

She wrinkled her nose at him. The area they were boating was less well traveled than others but there was never a shortage of tourists in Hawaii. Gabe was heading out into quieter waters but they had yet to leave civilization behind.

"You can't afford a boat. Even if you got one, the dock fees would kill you."

He shrugged. "For now. We won't be in school forever. Once I get my degree I can look into making real money."

"In Hawaii?" She couldn't help a skip of her heart. He had said he wanted to stay on the island chain but things could change.

It was then she understood that she had fallen in love with Gabe. This fire god descendant was all she wanted. She turned her head to the ocean and let the salt water strike her. She had never felt so alive.

"Yes. I love it here. Fire and water, perfect for both of us, don't you think?"

She held her breath but all he did was resume steering.

"Yes. I do think it's perfect for us."

Chapter 4

He wished he had the courage to speak but words failed him. Could he take the chance and admit that he'd been in love with her since the moment he saw her? The words beat inside him like small hammers. *I think it's perfect for us.* The words seemed so inadequate. They didn't say half of what he wanted to say.

The water sprayed him, dampening his clothes. He didn't have the enjoyment of the water like Emilia did but watching her turn her face to the spray was its own reward.

"Gabe, I'm so happy. Thank you for understanding this was the answer."

His heart stopped at the expression on Emilia's face. He was struck by a desire to hear her sing. She would be amazing in her siren form, singing as she was meant to. But that was up to Emilia. If she chose to honor him with her song, he would be happy to listen.

"I needed it, too," he admitted. He turned his attention to the wheel and looked into the distance. When they got out far enough he would idle the boat and then she would go to the ocean. For the moment he enjoyed the waves.

She barely made a splash as she entered the water, her gills forming and her tail thickening her legs until they were one long green and blue appendage. Using her now webbed hands and the flukes at the bottom of her tail Emilia descended to where she wouldn't be visible. Dolphins clamored for her attention and she called a greeting back. They lifted their noses in recognition. Sea lions joined them. There was a rich array of fish that darted this way and that in the warm waters. She detected sharks and at least one among them was a shifter. If it was Maleko he did not identify himself.

She swam, letting the water sink into her body, soothing her mind and her soul. Her eyes adjusted to the dim light and she marveled at the life around her. The ocean was never still, never boring. It teemed with more animals and plants than she could count. Nearby there was a coral reef and fish of all kinds darted through its protective arms. Emilia smiled.

She had no wish to return to the surface. She could stay down here, safe from terrible people like Rector. Down here she could exist without the strictures of so-called "civilization." She did not need to be among humans. She could be with those who understood her. Not awful demi-gods who would take away her freedom.

Emilia dove to the sea floor and flipped her tail along the bottom, sending sediment flying into the air. The dolphins chittered in a sound that was different than moments ago. Several headed up to breathe. A school of triggerfish clustered above her in a tight ball before darting this way and that, their school breaking up. She moved toward even deeper water, trying to elude the faint light above them. She wanted to be down in the depths, where man could not see her and she would be safe.

As she got lower, she saw several Hawaiian conger eels, who burrowed into the sand when they spotted her. She avoided the coral reef, afraid she might harm the delicate structure. She could make her home among a shipwreck on the deep ocean floor. She could make friends with the shifters who inhabited these waters. She wouldn't be alone.

There was no need to return to the surface. There was nothing but danger up there. Here it was safe.

Gabe struggled to remain patient while he waited. Emilia had been down there for what seemed like forever but was probably no more than a half hour. There was no way to help her in those dark waves, no way to go where she was going without bulky equipment. He was not trained in SCUBA and was at best an adequate swimmer. Water had never appealed to him.

He glanced at the sky where the sun was beginning to set. An uneasy feeling stirred inside him. If he was on land he might have felt the earth quiver but he had no power on the water. He squinted at the waves. Something moved…yes, there it was. He frowned.

"I keep seeing that boat," he said out loud. "It's been near us this entire trip."

He hadn't noticed it at first but as they went the other boats faded away but this one was never too far away. Not enough to be intrusive, but a little too close. He wished Emilia would return and they would head back. Now he wondered what he had been thinking to suggest this.

He went to the railing and peered to the spot where the other craft was. He tried to summon his fire power but nothing came to him. Dolphins capered around and sea lions were in the distance.

The other boat sped up, coming straight toward them. As it neared it cut its engines and slid alongside, its wake sending their vessel rocking. Gabe's worst fears were realized when he saw Rector.

"What the hell?" Gabe said, his face darkening with rage. "Get the fuck away from us, Rector."

They were close enough so that he could see the look on Rector's face, the evil grin that twisted his expression. He punched some buttons on the control panel and then leered at Gabe.

"I couldn't take the chance you were trying to escape. You left me no choice. It is her stubbornness that caused this. All she had to do was sing, but she wasn't going to do that. Bitch. I'll get to her in a minute. First, I have to deal with you."

As much as he had wished moments before for her to return, now Gabe hoped Emilia stayed away. He had to get the man away from where Emilia was. Gabe turned the steering wheel but it was too late. The boats scraped together. Rector ran to the back and opened his hands. He waved them in a circular motion and then appeared to hurl something down into the sea.

To his horror the underwater marine life started jumping out of the waves, their movements frenzied. A shark leaped high up and then splashed back down. A spinner dolphin heaved itself out of the water and hit the railing as it went back down.

Rector clapped his hands together. Panic washed over Gabe. His body was taut from the effort to keep from screaming. Dread surged through him and he started tearing at his life jacket. He flung it aside, then yanked at his clothes. A pygmy killer whale jumped out of the water, slamming onto the deck. His heart was beating so fast he thought it would vibrate out of his chest. The whale struck him and his feet flipped out from under him, sending him sliding. Despite his pounding heartbeat and the fright shooting through him he managed to regain his footing.

Run run run. His spooked brain told him to flee, to get away from there, but there was nowhere to go. He scanned the area, looking for something, anything, to get away.

Rector made that motion with his hands again. Terror jolted through Gabe and he reeled back from the impact of that sonic blast of horror coursing through him. He flailed around the deck, the panic coating his brain. His feet slid on the damp wood, then he stumbled and hit the railing.

And went into the ocean.

Emilia looked around at the sound of her name, both heard and yet not heard. A human would not be able to see without illumination, but she could.

Emilia.

She whirled around and saw a form standing a few feet away. For a moment she thought she was seeing things. He had the torso of a man but his legs were tentacles. They moved under him although he stood still, his body moving a little in the waves. He was dark haired and thick featured, and stared at her without wavering.

There was no doubt who this was. Her previous brief vision recently danced in her mind.

Kanaloa, you honor me. She wondered if she should bow or…what did one do when one met a god? She had no reference. In all her years on the island she had never seen him before, nor heard her mother mention encountering him.

Thank you, siren. It is indeed I, Kanaloa. Emilia, you must not stay down here.

She shook her head, feeling the currents eddy as she did so. Her tail waved behind her similar to how the god's tentacles moved.

Danger lurks on the surface. It is safer on the ocean floor. Rector would have no reason to hunt Gabe if she were not around. She could stay down here until Rector got bored and left, and then return. Gabe would understand.

The surface is not the only place danger lurks. Can you not sense the volcanos? They will erupt if you do not stop this. Quickly. There is not much time.

Now she did feel a tremor, something she had attributed to the sea bed. She cocked her head and looked at the god. Down here she was not afraid. Down here she was a siren and while they were not equal, she was not without her merits.

I thought you would want the land to come into the sea. She struggled to remember her Hawaiian mythology. Didn't you cause a great submerging a long time ago?

Kanaloa's tentacles waved in her direction. Two impossibly long appendages closed the distance until they lurked just beyond her. Emilia squeaked, aware that he could wrap these giant things around her and squeeze until she died.

There is truth to that legend but that means nothing. I have no wish to see this chain sink into the sea. It does me no benefit. Pele would lose her volcanos. She is precious to me. There is little time, siren. Even now the heir of Lyssa succeeds.

The heir of Lyssa…Rector is up there?

Her heart pounded. She could go deeper, so deep that nobody could find her. She turned to do it and then stopped. Something tickled the back of her mind. She felt the minds of the dolphins and sea lions and then heard echolocation as sound bounced toward her.

There is not much time. Every moment is a moment at risk. Emilia, siren, you must stop this.

But…Rector. He will come for me.

Some things are more important. Emilia, open your thoughts. Hear the world around you.

Then something fell like a dead weight. She stared in horror at the god.

Gabe!

Hurry, siren.

The god vanished as though he had never been there.

Gabe was plummeting too fast. There was no way he was swimming at that speed.

Gabe! She used all her mental abilities to try and reach him. She received no response.

Heart in her mouth, she focused on Gabe dropping through the water. His limbs were trailing upward as if he was trying to head back to the surface. Emilia shot toward her boyfriend, sending a few dolphins to intercept him. She could not tell if it was already too late.

As she got closer a shark positioned itself under Gabe, breaking his descent. Gabe bounced off the animal and would have continued down, but the shark neatly nipped his collar and pulled him to a stop. She sensed humanity in the shark. Gabe floated in the deep water, his hair waving, his clothes sodden, showing no signs of consciousness. Emilia reached him moments later. The dolphins crowded around, making distressed sounds.

The sandbar shark, judging by its hide and high dorsal ridge, slid Gabe onto its body. Her boyfriend rested against the fin and the rest of the shark. Emilia grabbed Gabe's arm. She met the shark's eyes and saw intelligence there. One of the dolphins nosed Gabe but he didn't stir.

Emilia had to get Gabe to the surface. He may have the blood of gods running through his veins but that didn't make him immune to drowning. He had no power in this medium. Without air he would soon be dead.

She gestured to one of the nearby dolphins to aid the shark. It got close to Gabe and then it too was under him, the two bodies supporting Gabe. Emilia pointed upward.

Together they headed for the rippling surface far above them. The sun was setting but there was still a bit of light. She had wished for darkness but now hoped there was some moon on this night.

In the distance she heard the volcano rumble. Gabe didn't respond, although she thought she felt him shudder in time to the volcano. The dolphins chittered in alarm.

They broke the surface as one entity, shark, dolphin, man and siren. To her relief the boat was only feet away. Emilia kicked toward it, feeling her gills and tail diminish as she willed them away. She saw the lights of what could only be Rector's boat a short distance away. She couldn't fathom what the lunatic was thinking. Perhaps the goddess of frenzy and her descendants were none too stable. She didn't have time to care. The sandbar shark transformed into Maleko who helped Emilia get Gabe on board. Emilia's heart raced at the sight of his still figure. She had never learned CPR, there was no need.

The man took Gabe and laid him flat and positioned himself over Gabe's ribs, gesturing to Emilia to begin mouth to mouth. Gabe was still and it was all Emilia could do not to cry. Together they worked on Gabe for a few heart stopping moments to no effect.

Then to her profound relief, her boyfriend heaved out a giant breath. Emilia turned his head to the side so Gabe could cough up the remaining water. It dribbled from his mouth and he sighed a shaky breath.

"What happened?" Emilia asked, her gaze going from Gabe to the shifter.

Maleko made a dismissive gesture. "It does not matter. Right now, there are more urgent matters to attend to. Haleakalā is angry. Pele is furious. So is the sea god. The great-grandson of Lyssa disturbs them all."

Gabe spit up more salt water, his breath coming in short gasps. To her relief, his eyes were clear. "Thank…you…" he wheezed.

"No time for thanks," Maleko said, pointing to where the rise of the volcano could be seen by the light of the setting sun.

It wasn't fair to ask Maleko for another favor, but rage filled her vision with the need to act.

"Can you watch things here for a few minutes? I have something I have to do."

"Yes, if you are going after the godling." Maleko pointed toward the other boat. Emilia nodded her agreement.

"I am."

"Good. You are not who Pele would have chosen for vengeance but gods are practical. A siren's song is a weapon that all fear. I will protect myself from your melody."

Before she could react, there was a thump and a grinding sound. Emilia yelped and jumped back. Her gaze darted to her left and she saw Rector's boat inches from theirs. He had come up on them on their blind side. She cursed at their inattention.

"You will give me what I want or I will kill your boyfriend," Rector said, his voice audible above the waves.

She heard a splash and moments later he climbed onto their boat. Rector's boat began drifting away from them.

Gabe got to his feet, his movements slower than she would have liked. He still looked a bit dazed, his face and body still wet with salt water. Maleko stayed at the captain's area, keeping the boat steady.

"Goddamn you, siren, you will sing for me now!" Rector lunged for Emilia. The light from his boat cut across their bow in a back and forth manner, swinging as his boat did, from one side to the other.

"Emilia, behind me," Gabe said and stepped in front of her, his large body blocking her from Rector's lunge. The other man growled. The boat dipped in the waves, the roar of the engine loud. "You don't get her song," Gabe spat. "You need to get off this boat. You are not welcome around us. Pele doesn't want you here. Can you feel the volcano? That is because you dare to disturb the Hawaiian gods."

"I do not care about the petty gods of these stupid islands. My pantheon is greater than theirs," Rector said and in the red light his face looked like a mask. "You will sing for me or I will post tomorrow. Then all the world will know what you are."

"You are a fool to ignore these gods," Gabe said and Emilia stepped out from behind him. He held an arm over her crossways.

A frantic look crossed Rector's face and his hands clenched at his sides. His face twisted, crunching up and then releasing. Then he let out a roar of pure rage.

Rector lunged for her and Gabe blocked his path. The boat rocked and Emilia put a hand on the railing. Spray from the ocean below hit her skin, making her begin her transformation into her siren form. She yearned to go into the water.

Rector's mouth opened wide.

Chapter 5

Gabe shut his eyes and liquid fire danced through his veins He looked at Rector, the man who would try to take his siren from him, and rage as potent as the lava that lurked far beneath the surface filled him. Pele swam into his vision, with a smile full of teeth.

Steam rose from the slick deck. His skin glowed with an inner fire. He stepped toward the would-be so-called god, and stretched out his hands. Rector had tried to claim his siren and that could not be borne. He would not allow this puny godling to get away with his actions. Rector would pay.

The boat continued to rock but it didn't matter. He would not be thrown off by a mere wave. Kanaloa's presence was not his to feel but he somehow knew that the water god did not object to him. Only Rector.

Gabe heard chittering below them and then Emilia was answering. Maleko made sounds as well, lower and more resonant, like the tones of the whales. Rector did not have the advantage on the water, but in his arrogance he thought himself better than all of them.

Snarling, Gabe faced Rector, flexing his hands as he did so.

❧ ☙

As Emilia watched, Rector advanced toward Gabe. She opened her mouth to lure Rector away, but her boyfriend waved his hand no.

"Don't give him that, Emilia. Your song is only for you. I will handle this."

"If I sing for him this all ends."

"Then you are giving him what he wants."

The volcano rumbled in the distance.

"You cannot stop her from singing," Rector cried. "She will sing for me whenever I wish it. I am a god. I do as I please. Come, foolish siren, you have wasted enough of my time. I would put you in a tank and you would sing when I will it. It is my right."

"The hell it is. She is nobody's possession."

Gabe launched at Rector and the other met him halfway. Gabe threw him to the ground and slammed his head into the deck hard. Rector leaped to his feet and came at Gabe again. The boat rocked just enough to make Rector stumble.

"I am a god too and you will not get what you want."

"You are no god."

Rector charged again and this time Gabe wrapped his hands around the other man. Emilia saw the red glow emanating from Gabe and heard a faint hiss of steam as their bodies met.

Gabe slammed their heads together and Emilia winced, but it did not seem to affect either. Rector clawed for his eyes but Gabe eluded the other man.

Out of nowhere a shark rose out of the water and managed to butt Rector, sending him tumbling to the deck. Emilia gaped at Maleko but all he did was smile.

Rector jumped up and lunged at Gabe again, who dodged him. "I will have her," he said. "Lyssa told me that I could have what I wanted."

"You will not. She is not a prize to be doled out. She chooses, not you. That is the way with sirens. Lyssa does not speak for them."

Emilia knew what she had to do. It was what she should have done in the first place, as she intended before the idiot leaped onto their boat.

He wanted her song and he would get it. She opened her mouth and sang a few notes. Rector fell silent with a stupid look on her face and Gabe and Maleko both stared at her.

"Go to your boat," she sang to Rector, in words meant only for him. "Go there and I will sing to you."

Gabe turned as though to obey but she pushed him back toward Maleko. Without hesitation Rector jumped in the water and swam toward his craft. Gabe and Maleko went to follow but she faced them.

"No. Do not follow." She sang to them only, a melody of staying and holding. When they subsided, Emilia marveled. She did not know until that moment the true power of a siren's voice.

She raised a hand to the men and returned to the sea, shifting to her siren form. The sea lions and dolphins arrowed toward the spot where Rector's craft was.

"I am coming for you, Rector," she said, closing the distance to Rector's idling boat.

When she got there, she rose out of the water, balancing on her tail. She gleamed in green and blue, her scales glittering. She opened her mouth and began her song, a plaintive wail of loss and tragedy. She hoped that the ones on board her boat were far enough away not to hear it, but the siren didn't care. Right now, all that mattered was getting her revenge on Rector, the man who dared to touch her love. Who dared to upset the local gods.

Rector came to the railing, his expression rapt. He stared to where she was balanced on her tail, her naked breasts and torso gleaming with water, her hair soaked. She was a creature of the sea, powerful and elemental, at one with her medium and the power it gave her and her song.

She sang and he swayed, his mouth open and eyes closed, a slavish look on his face. It was too easy to bring a man to her with her song. It was why she'd never sang to Gabe. She wanted to know that it was her he desired, and not her gift.

"Yes. Yes. This is what I need. My father said there is a world beyond imagining in your voices. I wanted your song. Now I have it."

She paused and tilted her head toward him and Rector groaned in dismay.

"More," Rector said. "More. I have to hear more."

Emilia smiled, the memory of Gabe's descent into the water searing across her vision. Dark anger filled her. Rector said that her song was what he wanted and he would get more than he could have ever imagined.

The melody coming from her mouth was a tale of melancholy weaved with hope, of longing and passion. Rector rocked toward her and she continued, weaving desire into her tones. There would be no resisting this siren's call.

Haleakalā rumbled and she thought she heard a goddess's voice in the vibration. Pele.

"Follow me," she sang and turned away, gliding across the water. After a moment the sound of the engine told her he was coming nearer. She wanted to wound the man who thought, in his arrogance, that being the great-grandson of a goddess was enough to ensure he could come to no harm. She was a siren and even gods were affected by their song.

"Stop, stop. I can't hear. I have to have it all."

She headed for the coastline. There was an inhospitable shore with Rector's name on it. He would pay for what he had done.

The dolphins ducked under the water. She saw humped figures moving in a line toward where she had last left Gabe. Emilia frowned but then shrugged. What the creatures did was no concern of hers. Even the shark shifter who had helped was irrelevant at the moment. All that mattered was her song—and vengeance.

"Wait, come back. I can't hear your song." Rector called, his voice plaintive. She continued to move toward the place where he would dash his craft against black volcanic rocks.

The light of Rector's boat shone on her, showing her blue and green scaled tail, and her webbed hands. Her hair waved around her back in heavy wet ropes. The gills at her neck were set off by the faint greenish gleam of her skin. Emilia shot a glance over her shoulder and saw Rector straining toward her. He appeared to want to leap out of the boat. No, he could not do that yet. Not until he was closer to the shore, where rocks lay piled up like jagged sentinels.

She slowed so that Rector would catch up. She did not need breath, she did not need air, all she needed was to sing. Her song was designed to defend as well as entice. No man could resist her.

She had been foolish to deny what she was.

One of the dolphins came up and pointed its nose at her. It shifted just enough so she could see human features under the dolphin hide. All around them was darkness and stillness, broken only by the sound of the waves and the songs of whales.

"Stop, siren," the dolphin said and he sounded elder, like a leader of the pod. She no longer cared if humans saw her. She was a siren and she shouldn't have to hide. She lifted her voice to start singing louder. Rector could not be allowed to escape her lure. He had wanted this; he had caused this and now he would pay.

Emilia paused and she heard Rector take a deep breath as though he was coming out of his trance. She sang again before he could come to his senses.

"More," was all Rector said. "I must have all of your song."

Kanaloa's voice rumbled through her as though it was part of her mind. That is enough, siren. There is no need for further vengeance. The boy will never be the same. We are satisfied.

Two tentacles poked above the water and then sank down below the waves.

She tilted her head and fell silent. Rector's cries rang out in the night.

"More song, more," he demanded. "It is as glorious as my father said. No wonder he died searching for a siren who would give him what he wanted. It was worth anything to hear your song. I must have more. I must have it. Why did you stop? Why are you so cruel?"

She had changed Rector irrevocably. It would be enough.

She paused for a moment, caught in the promise of life in the sea, where the petty worries of human life could not touch her. Part of her still wanted to go down there, where she would be safe. Kanaloa might like company. But it was a place Gabe could not follow and she could not be without him.

"You will get nothing more from me. I choose my companions. Gabe is my man, now and forever. He is the only one I want to be with. You are nothing to me." She sang a few more melodies, putting all her disdain and dislike for the demi-god into her discordant tune.

Rector shot her one more pleading look. She cast Rector a scornful glance.

"That is all you will ever hear. You are not worthy of my song."

As she disappeared into the waves she heard Rector's wailing behind her. She did not care. He was unimportant. Gabe needed her.

❧ ☙

I do not want the volcanos to erupt on my account.

The image of Pele flowing through lava in her red gown surfaced in his mind.

I am not sure I want to hold them back.

Pele didn't sound angry, she sounded amused. Part of him wanted to see them erupt as well in a blaze of ash, sparks and lava greater than any the islands had seen since they were born.

But that was would destroy everything. Gulping down a nervous breath, he focused on the goddess in his mind.

They must stop.

It is what they do. They honor you.

I feel more fortunate than you know but I would not see humans harmed.

Humans come and go. The earth lasts.

Yes, but human is what I am.

You are not.

Perhaps you are right. Yet I would not see them damaged.

Then talk to the volcanos. They act on your behalf.

Pele faded before Gabe could ask any more questions. He glanced at Maleko and then in the distance where he could see the looming outline of the volcano that made up much of Maui. He steadied himself on the rocking ship and reached out.

Great volcano, you honor me with your power. It is more than this humble fire descendant deserves. The siren is pursuing the one who would bring disgrace to our island chain. Kanaloa's helper will bring down the arrogant godling. Leave this to her.

There seemed to be a slowing in the rumbling, as if the volcano was considering his words. It did not speak as much as it answered in bursts of impressions. Ground. Waving. Lava. Sparks. There was fire deep down under the land. Haleakalā could reach down and grab that magma and awaken with a roar, spilling the contents of the earth into the air and earth. When the descendant of Lyssa dared to touch one of its fire gods, it hungered to act.

If Haleakalā erupted Maui would be destroyed. Gabe reached out to Pele but she slipped away. He had gotten all the help he would get from the goddess.

The boat dipped and he grabbed the railing. He was feeling better and thanked his god blood for his quick healing. He might need it against Rector if there was anything left of the other god when Emilia was through with him.

He sent soothing thoughts of quiet volcanos and peaceful times when humans and volcanos lived together in harmony, where the humans respected Haleakalā's power. Gabe reassured the volcano that none were his superior.

A few moments the volcano started to quiet, the rumbling lessening and the magma sinking back into the earth. The volcano rumbled one more time and subsided.

Gabe breathed a sigh of relief and looked around, trying to find Emilia.

"I need to go to her," Gabe said, seeing the light of Rector's boat closer to shore.

"You will not," Maleko said with a firm hand on Gabe's shoulder. "We are in Kanaloa's domain, not Pele's."

Gabe stared at the man he called friend, who was part fire god and part shifter. There was a lot about his adopted home he had neglected. If he was going to live here he needed to learn a great deal more about the culture.

"Kanaloa won't hurt Emilia, will he?"

He shrugged, a movement Gabe could barely see in the gloom. "Who knows the will of the gods?"

There was a ripple in the ocean and a cry from Rector's boat. It was a wail of loss and pain, of regret and intense loneliness. Rector's agony was so real that if it were anyone else Gabe might have felt sorry for him.

To his relief he saw Emilia speeding toward them.

❧ ❧

When she hauled herself onto the boat Gabe helped her in as though she was the most precious thing in the world. Naked and dripping with sea water, Emilia stood there, breathing fast.

"Emilia, are you okay?"

She nodded, and the look on Gabe's face eased.

"I am, but Rector won't be."

Maleko dropped a blanket around her and grunted. "I'm going to check on things," he said and Emilia turned her gaze to him.

"Thank you," she said, belatedly realizing her manners. "I, we, couldn't have done it without you."

"It isn't for you I did this, Emilia. My ancestors speak highly of the sirens. I am glad to meet one in person. But my reasons were more basic. The gods were angry and you two were their methods of revenge."

"Thanks," she said. Maleko nodded, his face unreadable.

"'*A'ole pilikia*. You're welcome."

Her gaze went to the dark shape of the volcano behind them. Goose bumps erupted on her forearms.

"What about you? Are you okay?" she asked, turning her attention back to Gabe.

"I'm fine, just mad at myself," he said, sounding chagrined. "I should have known that creep would follow us."

She smiled and put her hands on his shoulders. "It's over. He got what he wanted. I sang for him. I'm pretty sure he didn't like my song at the end but that's his problem. Oh Gabe, I was so scared. Are you sure you're okay?"

He cupped her chin and met her eyes. "I'm fine. I had my siren to protect me. Where is Rector?"

She waved a hand toward the shoreline in the distance. "I sent him that way. Even if he hits the rocks, he will probably survive. He is a god, after all."

Gabe kissed her then, as if he could not stop himself, relief and passion in that kiss. His lips moved over hers in a gentle caress, claiming and reassuring at the same time.

"It is more than he deserves."

She slid her hands around his waist, enjoying the warm feel of his skin under her palms. He would always run a bit hotter than other mere mortals and the touch of him reminded her that he was a god just as she was a siren.

"In the end it was Kanaloa who stopped me. I don't know why."

"The ways of the gods are strange," Gabe agreed. "I didn't really understand that until now. I may never understand but it doesn't matter."

There was no more rumbling from the volcano. It was apparently satisfied that the descendent of Lyssa was no longer a threat. Or perhaps Pele and Kanaloa had helped. It was hard to know anything for sure any more.

She held out her arms to Gabe and he enfolded her in his embrace. He raised a hand to the shark shifter. Maleko set course back to the marina and started off at a slow pace. The dolphins, sea lions and sharks flowed back into the depths of the sea, the dolphins calling a goodbye as they did so.

"Rector has convinced me that I need tell you the truth. Emilia, my siren, my woman, I love you. I know we've only been dating a little while but I've loved you from the moment I set eyes on you."

Emilia pressed a kiss to his lips and then drew back.

"I have wanted to hear those words since we first went to Maui together. You're so special to me, more than you know."

"And?" His prompt made her grin.

"And I love you back. You are everything I want and will ever want."

He kissed her, a slow promise of love and days to share together and lives to intertwine. Whatever happened next, she was where she was supposed to be.

❧ ☙

Rector was gone when they returned to classes. Emilia found out his great grandmother was at his apartment when he returned and there had been an argument of epic proportions. She had seen but a glimpse of the battle frenzy of Rector's and could not imagine what his pure-blooded great grandmother's rage would be like. She did not think things would go well for Rector for a while. She didn't know if his great grandmother would want to avenge herself on

Gabe and Emilia. If she wanted to try she was welcome to it. She had little doubt who would win that battle.

There were no further messages from Rector and nothing on his blog. In the end she had done as he asked. The bargain had been fulfilled. If Rector exposed her now it would be seen as bad faith and there were Greek gods who did not take kindly to oath breakers. She should be safe, at least she hoped so. She could never be sure, of course, but that was the nature of existence.

"Are you ready?"

Gabe's voice cut into her reverie. He slid his arm around her and tugged her to him. Classmates flowed around them, some waving and some intent on their business. Her friends who knew that Rector was pursuing her had made a few comments but mostly they let it go. As long as Emilia didn't make a big deal out of it the memory of the blogger at their school would fade.

"I'm done for the day, if that is what you mean," she said and placed a hand on his stomach. The fact that he loved her was overwhelming and magnificent at the same time.

"I thought we'd go get a picnic and go onto the volcano. I have some thanks to give."

She studied him for a moment. "Gabe, would it really have exploded?"

He shook his head in an uncertain movement. "I don't know for sure, Emilia. Pele is a fierce goddess. The Hawaiian gods do not tolerate intruders in their midst. Rector thought he was powerful but they are more than he can imagine."

"Yet they told me to let him live."

Gabe's touch was gentle. "I think that in the end the decision was yours. You are a siren and not subject to any man's claim. When faced with vengeance or mercy you chose mercy and they allowed it. Emilia, I am so happy you are mine."

She traced his face with a gentle finger. "As you are mine. Gabe, what do you think about a trip? This experience has made me think we need to go to Greece and Italy. I have an island of sirens to visit and it sounds like you may want to get an audience with your ancestor. Maybe we can see the famous home of the gods."

He shrugged. "Hephaestus will see me but I don't think I'll get an invite to Olympus. As you saw, the Greek pantheon thinks highly of itself. Let's do it. We have a lot to explore."

"Then it's a date," she said and they began walking together.

"What's next for us, Emilia?" Gabe pointed toward the ocean where the waves flowed into the sand. It was calm, for the moment. If she needed to she could summon the water and its creatures. Kanaloa might grace her with an appearance if she asked nicely.

"I don't know," she said. "I want to travel but in the end I want to live here."

He smiled. "That's what I want too. But it doesn't matter where I go, as long as you are with me."

Her heart fluttering at his words, Emilia said nothing for a moment. Then she flung herself into his arms and kissed him soundly.

"I feel the same. Oh Gabe, say it again."

He seemed to understand what she was asking. "I love you, Emilia. You are my woman and my siren, now and for the future."

"I love you back, my fire god," she replied and kissed him again.

Siren's Crush

Foreword

I wrote *Siren's Crush* for a now defunct publisher called Cheapjack Pulp. Cheapjack Pulp took a chance on one of my early romance stories (*Truth in Beauty*) and that particular publication can still be found online. However, at the time *Siren's Crush* was released Cheapjack Pulp was already in the process of making the hard decision to shut down, so there are no copies of it in that magazine available online.

The story may be familiar to some as I have been offering it as a free short story for members of my newsletter. I hope that the beginnings of Gabe and Emilia are as thrilling to read as they were to explore.

Siren's Crush

What you got there?” Gabe asked, pointing at the flaking green and purple thing propped in a corner of the living room.

Emilia schooled her face to reveal nothing. “Prop. Dean found it at a yard sale and thought it was hilarious. His big idea is to say he fished it out of the water and charge money for people to see it. It's stupid, like him.”

He fingered the replica and some green paint came off in his hand. Gabe rubbed his fingers and grinned at her. “I knew it. You're a mermaid.”

Siren, but they're often mixed up.

“Yep, that's me,” she replied, keeping her voice steady. “Mermaid all the way.”

“You do love the ocean,” he pointed out, looking out of their sliding glass door to the sliver of water that could be seen from their yard.

“So do you.”

He picked up a mango from the pile on the counter. Their tree was heavy with them at this time of year. One of the advantages of living in Hawaii.

“Ycah, but I'm not a great swimmer like you are.”

“Is there something in particular you wanted to do today?” she asked, making a mental note to get rid of the stupid mermaid tail when Dean wasn't looking.

Gabe shook his head, working on the fruit with a kitchen knife.

They had been school friends but she hadn't expected it to continue through the summer. But Gabe had surprised her with the text that he was staying on Maui for the break. With his shock of brown hair and eyes Gabe was on the cusp of turning from a dork to a handsome man guy and the girls at school had started to notice him when classes ended. Emilia had tried to ignore the pings of jealousy when another woman gazed at him. It was silly. Sirens weren't supposed to be jealous. They were the heartbreakers.

"I thought we could get a bite," he said with an eager smile.

"I'm not hungry yet."

"Fair enough," he enthused. "Up for a trip? What about the Road to Hana? I've always wanted to do that."

Emilia's heart leaped. Hana was a secluded area on the eastern side of the island, accessible primarily by a windy road. The beaches there were a combination of volcanic rock and sand, like most of Maui. There were many quiet spots where a siren could let her tail out.

"I've been to Hana many times. Mom and I love it there. There are lots of...art galleries...and we do the drive sometimes just to spend a day or two bumming around there."

Emilia gazed at Gabe, wondering what he saw when he looked at her. At five-six, with dark brown hair and a face that showed more her Midwest American dad's side than her mother's more exotic Greek beauty, Emilia had been told her hazel eyes and long lush mane of hair were her best features.

"Shall we do it?" Gabe said, brushing against her. For a moment it appeared as if he wanted to take her hand but he didn't complete the gesture. There was something comforting about Gabe, like a favorite pair of shoes or a family dog. But there was something else as well, a lurking passion that drew her like a magnet.

"I'm game for Hana," she said, glancing at the mountains and then out to the ocean where waves lapped until you couldn't see any more. The water called to her like the songs of her ancestors, ones they still sang to this day.

"*Mahalo*. I hear the road is challenging but the end result is worth it."

Emilia had kissed boys, but not many. There was always her secret between them, the fear that if she lost control she might transform into siren. Her mother assured her that that wouldn't happen, but the idea made her wary of getting into compromising situations with the opposite sex. Even men as appealing as Gabe.

"What about your folks?" he asked.

Emilia paused for a moment, wondering if Gabe was assuming too much. But she couldn't see anything on his face but concern and she relaxed. "They're gone to the big island for the weekend. We have property there." It had an enclosed pool where her mother could swim in her other form.

"And they won't mind you going away with me?"

"I'm an adult." She raised her chin at the suggestion that she was under her parent's control.

"You have an old fashioned family. Dean would take strips out of me if I took liberties with his sister. I can call them and reassure them that I'm trustworthy."

She blinked at the unasked for consideration. Although she was twenty-one her parents would worry if she took off with a boy. Even Gabe, who they had heard good things about, was still male.

"That would be great."

Her folks were worried but calmed down when Gabe reassured them that he would behave. They trusted him, sight unseen. He had that effect on people.

He had a different effect on her. She found herself wishing he wouldn't be so careful, but that was ridiculous. She couldn't share her secret with him so how could she hope for a relationship? It was fantasy.

"Let's go."

The Road to Hana, aka Hawaii Route 31, or the Piilani Highway, was fifty-two miles of small two lane road that narrowed down to one lane on forty-six of the fifty-nine bridges travelers had to cross to reach their destination. In those cases, whenever you came to a bridge you had to make sure there was no oncoming traffic before proceeding. There were lights and signals to help guide cars, who were forced by the terrain to take the curves slowly. Those fifty-two miles took two and a half hours to get there from Kahului, the main retail center of the island.

Gabe seemed content to look at the scenery and surf on his phone as they made their way to the small community at the edge of Maui. All around them was lush greenery, the trees forming a hushed canopy over the road. In some spots the vista opened out to spot the crashing ocean far below their path. In others waterfalls could be seen in the distance, splashing over huge boulders.

"I'm getting crap cell reception here but I managed to find a couple of hotels."

Emilia made a non-committal noise. They were staying overnight to enjoy the town, but her parents warned Emilia to be careful. She promised she would but wasn't sure she could live up to that vow. No boy before Gabe had ever made her feel like sunshine and happiness combined. Back in Michigan when she was younger and stupid she'd shared her secret with a boy she liked. He didn't believe her but got the other kids to call her crazy Fishmilia. They moved to Maui after that. Three people knew the truth now, and they were all related to her.

Telling Gabe wasn't an option, although she wished it was.

They passed Wailua Falls, one of the more spectacular waterfalls and Gabe raised an eyebrow, making a camera clicking motion with his hands.

"No thanks," she said and dabbed at the back of her neck with her sleeve. She had the air on full blast but it was hot in the car. Not muggy like the outside but the kind of heat you would get with a fire.

"I just had this A/C serviced," she said, frowning at the equipment. "It must be the road. Or it's you. You are always burning up."

Gabe's hands fell to his lap where he pressed his palms together in a tight grip. Emilia caught the motion and frowned. His face and body had gone still as if he were a statue.

"It's got to be the drive. It's too much for your little car." He coughed and looked out the window, presenting her with his profile.

Emilia said nothing, filing away his odd reaction for the future. She cranked up the A/C and went back to focusing on the road.

❧ ☙

After a stop for coconut water at one of the local stands, they continued for another hour until they reached the town of Hana. The town had once had six sugarcane plantations but was now shops and hotels. Rolling down the window, she felt the wind on her face and smelled the welcome tang of salt air just a few blocks off.

"Where should we go?" she said when they headed for the street parallel to the ocean. Gabe pointed toward a hotel ahead of them, jutting against one of the natural coves.

"I did some checking and found an app with discount hotel rates," he said. "We could go back in the morning. We shouldn't just turn around and leave. Your folks said we'd have more fun and they trust me. I told them I'd take care of you. We should take our time. It's break. We've got nowhere to be."

"But...this is expensive," she said, eyeing the three story rustic wood structure with its small fish ponds. The water was rough and thick with volcanic rocks here. Perfect. Sirens liked to sit on rocks and sing.

"Like I said, I got a good deal. What do you say?"

Gabe was still waiting for an answer. Emilia let her breath out in a rush. She could slip down to the ocean in the middle of the night. It was too tempting to pass up.

"We can stay."

❧ ❧

The one bedroom was small and open plan, with a small kitchen and a lanai. In this hotel there was little to distract you from unplugging and getting away, no TVs, no radios, nothing to take away from enjoying the moment. Of course they both had smartphones and Internet access if they wanted. They decided to stay in the spirit and played hands of gin rummy instead of surfing the net. She kept looking at Gabe's full mouth and lanky body, his heat drawing her like sunshine to a flower. He could keep her warm as the night grew colder. She shivered, a ghost image of him kissing her making her want to touch her lips with her fingers.

Raindrops thrummed on the roof, cooling down the muggy air. They had the doors open and the breeze brought a few drops heading their way, a welcome relief from the humid July weather. It had been a culture shock to go to a tropical rainforest from the Great Lakes region they'd lived in but Emilia adjusted. The year round swimming helped with that transition. She should thank that long ago boy she had confided in. Now there was Gabe, who was here for school but after that?

"Gin!" he proclaimed, showing his cards before giving her a smug look.

"Heyyyy," she said. "That's five in a row. No fair."

"My grandpa is the whiz. Nobody can beat him. He's won tournaments. He's played for so many years he is almost unbeatable." Gabe skittered to a stop, a flush crawling over his cheeks as if he'd been about to say something he hadn't meant to.

"Tournaments? Is there footage online? I'd love to see."

Gabe went taut, every muscle of his body clenched. He hadn't moved but he seemed far away.

"Nah, it was a long time ago," Gabe said, his voice sharp. "There's no moon until almost dawn today. Do you want to look at the stars?"

She wanted to know what Gabe had been about to say but his shuttered look told her he wasn't sharing. She was reminded that she was alone in a hotel room with a strange boy who she didn't know well. If he had secrets, then that was fine. She had the biggest secret of all. Let him keep his counsel about his grandfather, she didn't care.

"No, I think I'm done. I'm going to go to bed." She flounced into the bedroom. Shutting and locking the door, she stripped off her day clothes and put on the sweats she had bought at the local supermarket over an "I heart Hana" t-shirt that Gabe had paid for. Fine. He could pay.

Emilia punched the pillows and then rolled over to go to sleep, offended by the way he had shut down. It stung deep inside. Maybe she shouldn't trust him. Maybe she'd been a fool to come here.

She listened for a time until there was the telltale click of the lamp being turned off, followed by complete darkness. She would wait until she was sure he was asleep. Then she would slip out and go down to the water. Her heart pounded with anticipation of the cool water against her tail.

❧ ❧

Emilia paused at the sleeping form of Gabe sprawled on the too-small sofa, his legs dangling off the end and his arm flung over his head. She tiptoed past him, and out of the room. The creak of the wood stairs made her freeze, but after a moment nobody peeked their heads out from their room, or any of the rooms. This hour between late night revelers and morning surfers was the perfect time for her to stretch her gills.

The surf crashed against the black rocks on this rocky part of the cove. It was not an area for humans to be swimming, but it would suit a siren. If questioned later she would say that she'd wanted to go to the beach that could be seen in the distance and decided to take the direct way over the volcanic rocks. Anything was possible if you lied with a straight face.

She left her clothes in a pile on one of the lounge chairs, and eased onto one of the bigger rocks. Careful to check again for strangers, she slipped off her suit bottoms, leaving her top on. She then slid her naked torso into the rough sea but still clung to the rock. The change began at her waist, scales erupting on her body, replacing skin and moving down, fusing her legs until her bottom was one long, tapering glide of green and blue. The last thing to form was her large flip fin, radiating out from what had been her feet in a span three feet across. Her eyes began changing and Emilia dropped into the water.

Even before her gills erupted on her neck Emilia headed into the murky shadows, her vision clearing with every stroke. Rocks dotted the shallow water and she struck out toward deeper ocean, her tail gleaming behind her in a blue and green riot of color.

Fish slid around her, boxfish, angelfish and butterfly fish, their blues, greens and yellows now discernible with her improved vision. This close in there weren't any dolphins but she could hear them in deeper water calling to each other. After a moment they sent her a greeting via echolocation and she replied in kind. Humans were beginning to understand how intelligent this particular species was. There were many things that land dwellers had no inkling of. Even with their equipment they could not plumb the secrets of the ocean. She hoped it would always remain that way.

She didn't know how long she swam, but when she glimpsed the moon starting to wane toward the west she realized it had been hours. She could stay in there all day, and be happy. But she couldn't. She needed to get back before Gabe woke up. This was her private moment. It made her sad that she couldn't share it with a man. Even her human father was forever on the outside of this world, appreciating but not understanding.

Emilia waited as her tail shrank into legs in reverse from its formation. First the fin became feet, then the scales receded and the tail separated, leaving her as a two legged creature again. Then she hauled herself back onto the rock and slipped her bottoms on. After that she picked her way back across the rocks to the hotel grounds.

"Have a nice time?"

Gabe. Emilia spied him standing next to the lounge chair where she had left her clothes. Heart pounding, dizzy with fear, her mind raced through her available options. She could plunge back into the ocean, reform her tail and swim home. She'd have to figure out her purse and stuff later but maybe her father could convince Gabe to return them. Then she would have to leave Maui, get far away. Maybe she'd go to the siren's island and vanish. Nobody who wasn't invited could find that place. She would be safe there.

Gabe stretched his arms out toward her. The only sounds were the crashing of the waves, and the distant susurration of crickets. Although they were feet from the hotel, they might as well have been alone.

"Don't run, Emilia. I'm not going to hurt you."

Giving him another side-eyed glance, Emilia moved to where he stood. Her legs were slippery as if she still had scales and a fin. It was always that way for a few moments after her transformation back to human. Her neck still felt as it had gills. Emilia almost reached up but let her hand fall away.

The night air was cool and goosebumps rose on her arms. Once she made it to the sparsely grassed grounds, Emilia stopped. Gabe stood, his face still in shadow, holding out her sweatshirt.

Biting her lip, Emilia paused before hurrying to Gabe and snatching the shirt from him. She pulled it on, shivering as warmth replaced ocean chill.

"You..." She'd been about to say "you know what I am." No point in revealing herself if he were bluffing. She waited, arms crossed, until he handed her the loose fitting sweat bottoms.

Even through the fear Emilia appreciated his lean body in his own pair of sweats. His hair was tousled like he'd rolled out of the bed and come down here when he found her gone. Maybe he had. His heat struck her in a wave, making her shiver with welcome warmth. Under different circumstances she'd be thrilled to be alone with him.

"Come, let's sit," he said, helping her into the lounge chair as if she were a fine piece of china and plopped down in the one next to hers. Gabe gave her a look she couldn't interpret.

"You...you know..." she stopped.

The wind lifted his hair in a gentle breeze and Gabe pushed it back off his forehead. Now she could pick out his eyes in the bright moonlight, but not his expression.

"My great-great-great," he paused and raised his hands, fingers splayed. "Let me see. Great," he lowered a finger, "great," he lowered another finger, "great," another one went down, "great," a fourth one until all that was left was the thumb. Then he tucked his thumb in and lowered his hand. "Some number of greats-grandfather, said that the way to tell a supernatural being was in the way they reacted to their element. I knew the moment I saw you by the ocean what you were. It was a matter of figuring out if you were mermaid or siren." He smiled. "If you know where to look you have marks on your neck where your gills are."

A flush crawled up her face at the knowledge that she hadn't been the only one to see the faint lines. "Nobody has ever noticed those before. What did you decide?"

"Siren," he said without hesitation. "I've heard you sing."

She was glad for the cover of darkness. "Yes."

"He said that sirens are proud creatures and guard their privacy. He also said you were worth it."

An image of his hand folding down the fingers flashed across Emilia's mind. He had used them all and that hadn't been enough.

"Who is he? How does he know so much about sirens?"

Gabe reached out his hand to her, palm up. Trembling, Emilia placed her hand in his. His hand was warm, almost hot, and the heat sank into her chilled flesh. Emilia shivered, goosebumps rising again.

"That's what happens when your great-whatever grandfather is Hephaestus. I have lost count of the generations but of course he doesn't age."

She blinked, looking like one of the blow fish she had seen underwater. "Hephaestus, the Greek god of fire?"

His smile widened until she could see the moon gleam off his teeth. "That's him."

"You're a god? An immortal?" She glanced up to the dark panes of glass above them but nobody moved.

"I suppose I am a demi-god," Gabe said. "But that was many centuries ago. After a few generations the immortality, along with god-like powers, stopped. I'll live longer than a regular human, like you, but I'm not immortal."

There was a glow of red from his index finger and the fire pit behind them caught. Now she could see his face and his expression was mischievous while also looking concerned.

"I'm the same Gabe I was when you went to bed last night. I told you we all have secrets."

She studied his face looking for malice, but couldn't see anything but concern. "I thought you were trying to get me to tell you mine, not that you were a god."

"I'm not. I have some weak powers but not enough to get an audience with Zeus, if I wanted. Which I don't. I hear he's a dick."

Emilia's lips twitched at the description of the primary god of the Greek pantheon. When her mother talked about the gods it was to paint Aphrodite and Demeter in an

unflattering light.
Gabe turned their clasped hands over and kissed her skin. His lips, like his hand, were warm. The heat of his body replaced the cool night air.

"Does it change things?"

Gabe had always shone where others paled by comparison. "Only in the best ways. I couldn't tell you. I wished you were different like me so I could be with you."

"I wished for it too. So much."

He tugged her up, rising to his feet at the same time. He was bathed in red and yellow from the fire, and was looking at her with such tenderness a blush crept over her cheeks. A man could lust without emotion, and although his ancestor was not a frivolous god like Dionysus didn't mean that Gabe would be serious about a siren. Just because he revealed himself didn't follow that he wanted a girlfriend.

"I came to Hawaii for the volcanos. It was a perfect place to be able to experiment with my ancestry, but there was this beautiful woman in my math class. She had an affinity for the ocean, as I did for the volcanos. I'd met seen anyone like her." His free hand came up to caress her cheek, sending shivers dancing across her skin. "I couldn't find the words to tell you you were special."

She leaned against him, his heat coursing through her body. Maybe he wouldn't count for much to the gods but screw them. He counted to her.

"Oh Gabe, I had no idea. Why didn't you say something?"

He tilted her head up to his and grazed his lips over hers. His breath caught and then he was kissing her again, his arms pulling her across his body. His chest rose and fell quickly as if he had run a race. His hand held the back of her neck still as he tasted her. Emilia responded, pressing against him and feeling him tighten all over.

"I just did. I hoped you would choose me. If you knew how much I've dreamed of this moment."

"Me too," she said and kissed him again. Then she frowned. "I have to be close to water and you're the descendant of a fire god. How's that going to work?"

He gestured out to the cove, where the waves lapped against both rock and sand. "We're on an island created by volcanos. There is fire and water here."

"It's perfect," she agreed, a smile tugging at her lips.

"Let's watch the stars for a while," he said. "This doesn't need to happen all at once."

When the time was right, she would tell him what lay in her heart. She had reason to hope the feelings were returned. There would be words to be spoken. Love was on the horizon. It was as inevitable as the tide, as perfect as a seashell.

"Thank you," she said, pulling him back down to the lounge chairs. A feeling of protection washed over her as she was cradled in his arms. "It won't keep you waiting long."

"You're worth it."

She would never be Fishmilia to this man. A demi-god and a siren seemed unusual on the surface, but it wasn't.

It was meant to be.

Foreword

Finally, *Rising Melody* is a siren story unlike the other two. This was actually the first siren story I wrote when I became entranced with sirens. This was for a call for submissions about sirens and while the story wasn't selected for that anthology, it subsequently was selected for the first edition of Phantaxis Magazine, and published in November of 2016.

In this story I focused on the idea of the sirens' ability to sing. What if there was one who could not carry a tune? The rest of the story, including her brother, flowed from there. It was one of my early tales but I was already interested in exploring gods, and mythical creatures, and the possible mixtures of the two. I hope you enjoy this story of a winged and non-musical siren.

Rising Melody

Soaring above the clouds, her feathers waving and the wind in her hair, Rena glided. Down below, her mother Raidne was nothing more than a speck on a sea full of rocky dots. Rena knew she had been out too long. Mother would be mad. Sighing, she landed near the house and folded her wings.

To a casual observer there would be no age difference between mother and daughter. Raidne was an important Siren from legend, while her daughter didn't even have a footnote in history. She could not be found in any stories about the legendary females.

"You missed your singing lesson," her mother said, side eyeing Rena. "How do you expect to learn if you avoid your teacher?" A short, clipped series of notes followed her words, like a military march.

There had never been a siren who couldn't sing. It was part of who they were, the great mythology of their kind. Whether winged, like her, or aquatic, all sirens had one thing in common. Music. Except for her. At seventeen she couldn't hold a tune any better than she could when she was a child.

Some argued that her ability to fly was the reason she could not sing. The legends about why sirens had wings but no flight were as varied as the sirens themselves. The truth, as with most mythology, was somewhere in the middle.

"Mother, I would not be able to sing if Orpheus gave me lessons."

Raidne shuddered. "Do not mention that man." She flipped her raven hair back and hummed one single low bass tone.

It was said history was written by the winners. The sirens had wound up the villains in Greek mythology by the men who wrote the tales. Orpheus slipping back later to the bed of one of the sirens would not have been as popular as the saga of the lyre player who outplayed the women. Much like the tale of Odysseus was told that he was lashed to his mast to resist their song. That was not quite the truth. There had been lashes, to be sure, of a different kind.

All sirens sang. It was who they are. Rena, the first siren to be able to use her wings in hundreds of years, had only been gifted with one talent and it was not song.

"We have a guest for dinner," her mother said, her eyes sparkling. "A friend is visiting."

No outside boats had docked that day. Rena gave her mother a puzzled look, but the other woman said nothing.

The man in front of them had a wingspan twice the length of his body, creating shadows around him. He had a powerful build, almost like a bull, with thick shoulders and corded muscle across his back. It made sense for a Lamassu to look that way. It was not a lovely physique, but the immense dark chocolate brown wings made up for it.

"Rena," her mother said, gesturing to the man. "This is Panos." A tonal scale accompanied her words.

There was displeasure in the appraising gaze Panos turned on her. "I saw you fly. You lack proper form."

"Do not be disrespectful, Panos." Raidne said sharply. "She is a siren. Flight is not natural to her." Her vocal music faltered.

"Mm," he said in a non-committal tone. "I have not heard her sing. I have seen her fly." He murmured something under his breath.

Rena's wings lifted as anger burned under her skin. "I fly very well," she said with controlled fury. "Better than I sing."

Panos skewered her with a look that had her top feathers standing upright. "Let me hear you sing, and then I will judge."

Rena looked to Raidne, who nodded at the guitar in the corner.

"I will accompany you."

There were a variety of instruments in the house for the myriad times when sirens dropped by. Songs were all around them, in the other houses and common areas of the island.

"Sing 'Greensleeves,'" Raidne said and gave Rena a small nod. "Do not keep Panos waiting."

"I don't want to sing," she protested. The look in her mother's eyes made Rena shrug. "You'll be sorry," she said to the man who waited at the table, an expectant look on his face.

Panos winced as she stumbled through the verse. Even to her ears, she was failing miserably, the notes off-key, her voice shrill.

"Stop, stop," he said as she started on the chorus. "I agree you cannot sing," he said and gave Raidne a look. "She should learn to fly."

Raidne raised her hands and spread them out. "She is a siren. She sings."

"She is tone deaf." He gestured to Rena, who flexed her wings.

"Mother, why is this man talking to you in this manner? Who is he to us?"

Raidne smiled a sad smile. "Oh child, it is time you knew. He is your brother."

❧ ❧

Rena blinked. "Brother?"

Men visited but did not stay on the island. She had heard from time to time that boys were born of such unions, and taken away. He must be one of those. She could not see any resemblance. He was just a big Lamassu, with a beautiful pair of wings that made the rest of him tolerable.

"Brother?" she said again. She looked from his face to his torso, flexing one wing to compare it to his. Hers were smaller, but the same rich color. "How could a brother of mine be a Lamassu?"

Her mother gave her a knowing look. "You will learn the way of it. He is a Lamassu because his father was a Lamassu." She sounded three striking whole notes. "As you are a siren because I am."

"Why are you here?" Rena demanded. "Why have I never heard of a brother before?"

Panos looked at Raidne as if he was wondering the same question. Her mother shrugged.

"It is not spoken of. Men do not live among us."

Rena turned to her brother. "What am I missing?"

Panos smiled without mirth.

"If you cannot sing, you need to learn how to fly. I sent for him. Now I doubt the wisdom of my action." There was nothing musical accompanying Raidne's words; an unusual occurrence. "Sirens are not for flying."

"She is not for singing." Panos retorted, gesturing to the guitar.

"Excuse me," Rena said. "I'm right here."

"Yes," her brother said and met her eyes. She saw the resemblance in the seafoam green of his eyes and the tilt of his nose. His paternal DNA registered dominant, but traces of her mother were there, in the corners of his mouth and forehead.

"What do you propose?" she asked.

"Rena," her mother said, one low note vibrating in her throat. "Panos and your father can teach you flight, but you would need to leave. You have until tomorrow to decide." Again the tonal scale, as if that was how Raidne thought of her brother.

Men could not stay on their island. It hadn't been malice that made the sirens sing to the sailors. They had been lonely, banished to this small spar of rock to live out their lives. They were now allowed visitors, men who slipped in and left before morning light. Rena supposed that boys, even siren sons, also could not stay.

Her mother trilled a short note of exasperation. "We will speak no more of this tonight. You will have to decide, but that is for tomorrow."

Rena bowed her head, but her eyes moved to her brother. Her heart quivered at the thought of learning how to use her wings. Flight was within her grasp.

❧ ☙

"Psst."

Rena stirred, a breeze wafting over her, though she was sure she had closed the window before going to bed. The curtains blew in the wind.

"Psst," she heard again and jerked awake. There was a form in the rocking chair that rested in the corner of the room. It could only be one person.

"Panos," she hissed, darting a glance to the open window. "What are you doing here? What time is it?"

"It's five am," he said, his teeth glinting in the moonlight. She couldn't see his eyes in the gloom but she could perceive his powerful Lamassu form. A brother was a novel concept. She had sisters scattered around the island, but no males. She had had little male contact other than the day laborers and an occasional glimpse of the older siren's night visitors.

Not all sirens had the lifespan her mother and the primary sirens had. Nobody knew how long they would live, but few had died from the time of myths. It happened, of course, but by accident. Later sirens like her were not so fortunate. Their lifespans were indeterminate, depending on their mother and the strength in their sire.

"What are you doing here?" she asked again, flipping on a light. Panos' wings flexed and hers danced behind her in response, poking into the headboard. Rena yelped.

"It will be sunrise soon," he said pointing to the horizon and the faint streaks of dawn. "I thought you might want to see it from the air."

Her heart thumped in her chest, and her wings responded, fluttering behind her. He chuckled at her response.

"I think that's a yes, sister."

She bowed her head. "I should not, Panos. I should sing and not fly. Perhaps I will improve if I practice." She looked at him. "Did mother mean it when she said I could go with you?"

He gestured out the window again. The stars were fading, being replaced by the growing light of the morning sun.

"I cannot sing," he said and his tone was wistful. "My father wanted me to sing, it's why he lay with a siren. But I have no talent for it either. I am a good flyer. Our wings have lots of uses. The sirens should not be trying to make you into something you're not."

The pink hue that signaled the arrival of dawn grew. "We are sirens. It's what we do."

"It is time for new thinking. That is why your mother sent for me. That is why she has agreed to consider our request. Come, sister," he said, and extended his hand. "Let's fly."

❧ ☙

She banked and soared, watching Panos as he used the elements to control his flight, the wind a tool under his capable wings. She had always fought the gusts, not knowing how to glide with them. It seemed a simple thing now that she saw it done.

"You have much to learn, sister," Panos said, pivoting in a neat turn and pacing backwards with her as she went forward. Rena flushed, wanting to protest, but knowing he was right.

"Sirens do not fly," she said, trying to execute a similar turn but looping high as a current caught her and tumbled her over. It took Rena long moments to recover. All the while her brother waited, hovering, as she brought herself back.

"Nonsense," Panos said. "Things are changing. We no longer need fear the gods."

"Will you teach me how to pivot like that? It is like you are standing still."

"I can teach you," he said. "If you choose to come I can show you many things."

Rena sighed and folded her wings, heading straight down. Panos followed, his wings flat across his back. He plummeted past her and then pulled up, unfurling his wings between one breath and the next. She tried a similar action, but less successfully.

"Do you hear that?" she asked, cocking her head as she heard the lilt of music from below. "It is time for morning singing. I should be there."

"Sister," Panos said and his wing grazed hers. "Your flight is untrained but that can be corrected. You will never be a singer."

She flushed, but did not contradict him. She had been perversely proud of her lack of singing ability, until her new brother arrived.

"It is what we are," she said. Her feathers drooped.

"It is part of what you are, but it is not all of who you are. I understand your hesitation. It is hard to leave your home. Still, if you want to fly, you must. You will not learn here."

❧ ☙

Music wafted up to them from the island. Each siren had their own personal tune and all blended in a harmonic resonance throughout the landmass. The harmony faded away as they landed.

"I should go," Rena said. "I need to make breakfast. Mother will be mad that I did not sing this morning."

Panos fell into step behind her. "You worry too much."

She wanted to smack this upstart brother of hers, the boy she hadn't known existed until yesterday. It was one thing to know it inside your heart, and another for him to say it.

"It is time for new ideas," he continued. "Our father has sent me to school on the mainland. There are many interesting things to know. Humans do not see our wings. To them we look normal." Rena knew this. Tradespeople and shopkeepers came from inland and they did not comment on the siren wings or tails.

"Do you not feel the Lamassu inside you as well as the siren? You are a siren, but so much more. Like me. We are both products of our mixed heritage."

They walked in silence for a moment as Rena pondered his words.

"I am not convinced that mother will allow this, despite what she says."

They kicked up small puffs of soil on the dirt path. The singing had subsided, leaving the clank of dishes and the scents of breakfast behind. It was a quiet, rural life, on this island. If her mother wanted Rena to live this life as a siren, she was going about it all wrong. Rena did not understand why Raidne had sent for Panos. Perhaps Rena had misjudged her. Not every siren would lay with a Lamassu.

Panos looped his arm through hers. The sirens that were out stopped to stare at the man. What had those who explored the other realm of the outside world thought when they first got to the mainland? The noise and bodies must have been overwhelming. She had never experienced such a thing. Rena wanted to know.

"How do others of our kind exist in the human world?" she asked, flexing her wings until they stood up from her back. Their weight pulled her off balance and she smoothed her gait.

Panos grinned. "You will find out, sister. We live in Greece again. My-our-father was sad to give up his temples in Iraq but the region is unsafe for us. Much is being ruined by the humans. There is room for you if you wish to come and learn to fly."

They neared the house. Now that she was faced with the decision, Rena balked at leaving the island and everything she had known. The community was her source of support, the only thing she knew. And yet she could not deny the tug to explore the realm outside of her small confines of rock and ocean.

"Raidne would be lonely without me," she said.

"Sister dear she has been prepared for this day since she sent for me. Things are different in these times. What was once forbidden is now becoming more commonplace. Others have left. You have seen it. You speak from fear, not reality."

"What if I did? What would I do in the world? I have no skills. I cannot sing and I do not know what else there would be for me to do. Here I am safe. I have a place."

He shook his head, his thick neck barely moving. She and marveled that brother and sister could look so dissimilar and yet be alike.

"I do not know my father," she said and Panos grinned.

"I do not know my mother," he replied. Raidne hovering in the doorway, looking at them with something like regret in her eyes. "I cannot stay, sister. I must go within the hour. If you would come with me, gather your things. I leave after breakfast. I wish I had more time, but…" he gestured around. "Men do not linger on this island. It is the way of things. Perhaps someday it will be different. You would learn how to fly properly. Please consider it."

Rena nodded, looking wistfully at the sky.

❧ ☙

"I do not want you to go," Raidne said when Rena entered the house. Panos stayed outside. If Rena was to join him she would meet him at the highest spot on the island in one hour.

"Would you stop me?"

Raidne let forth a beautiful aria of sound, sliding up and down the scale in a minor key. Rena wished for nothing more in that moment to have the same ability. She could not sing yet she was a siren. Just as her mother had wings and could not fly.

"Why did you never tell me I had a brother?" Rena pressed and her mother broke off the song to murmur a few discordant notes before subsiding.

"It is not our way." She picked at a flaky croissant that lay on the table in front of her. "We do not discuss the boys." She made a sound like a jangle of dissonant cymbals. "You have never had the touch," she said, a mournful series of notes falling from her lips. "I thought it would be different when you grew older but it wasn't. I admit that you will never be able to sing." Again that tonal scale, followed by a brief soaring melody that Rena knew was hers alone.

"I am sorry, mother," Rena said bowing her head.

"Your father was a charming, gruff man. Panos takes after him. As do you. I know there is nothing to stop you going. You want to go. I have seen you fly." She belted out a wild series of notes. Rena felt the hush around them, the appreciation of the other sirens for a beautiful musical creation.

"I feared this day would come from the time I realized you had no talent. It has never happened in the history of the sirens. A girl without the ability to sing! We expect it of the boys but never the girls."

"I am sorry I'm a failure, mother," Rena said, her face coloring.

"Oh child," Raidne said and took Rena into her arms. She made a low lament of distress and pain. "You are not a failure. You are different."

After long moments her mother pulled back. Stroking Rena's hair, she smiled, but her eyes were sad. "I know you wish to go with your brother. Flight is a gift I cannot give you." She lifted her wings, with their bedraggled sparse feathers. It was one of the few things that were not beautiful on the sirens. In some ways their seagoing sisters were luckier. They at least had their tails and the ocean. After a moment, Rena looked into her mother's eyes and nodded.

"Yes. I do wish to go with Panos," she said.

She packed, and her mother arranged for more of her things to be sent to her father's house outside of Brasiae, located near Mount Taygetus. There, in the Taygetus mountain range, Rena would be able to soar off the mountaintops and into the valleys below. It seemed like paradise.

The entire island turned out to sing a song of mournful farewell as Rena and Raidne walked to meet Panos at the top of the island. The sea sirens had not joined the parade, but their voices could be heard from below.

Her palms itched with the idea of all she would be learning. She hoped her Lamassu father was a good teacher. Her life was about to change. She would never be the same again. She looked forward to the changes at the same time she was scared.

Rena took a final look at the gathered cluster of sirens and embraced her mother. Raidne's arms were tight around her daughter. Tears were in her eyes when she stepped back. Rena smiled, the ache in her heart a sharp pain. Then she stepped back, lifted a hand in farewell and turned to her brother. Together they unfurled their wings.

"Time to fly," she said.

Fire Danger

Special Preview

Foreword

As an added bonus, here is an excerpt from my first Elementals' Challenge book *Fire Danger*. While this story does not involve any of the characters in the siren stories I like to think that all of my paranormal tales could rest comfortably in the same world side by side whether they reference the events of any of the other narratives or not. I hope you enjoy this look into the story of the fire Elemental Phoenix and the half-Ifrit Rachel who is not only his love but possibly humanity's salvation.

Fire Danger Special Preview Chapter 1

"Stay back!"

The whoosh of his wings manifesting startled Phoenix, knocking him off-balance. They gathered behind him, sticking up from his body. Phoenix immediately crouched, his hands in front of him, trying to identify the cause of the danger.

His wings had so consumed his attention that it took him a minute to realize there was a voice in his mind that rang through like a bell. He jerked to a standing position.

"Get away from me!"

The mental voice was shrill and panicked. His wings unfurled fully, looming like large orange-and-red shadows above him.

"Dogs. Scary dogs. Too close. Snarling. Stay away from me."

Not his danger.

His workout DVD was no longer an option. Phoenix pressed Stop on the player, simultaneously reaching out with his mind to find the source of the signal.

"Big dogs. Too big. Run. No, don't run. They'll chase you."

The voice inside his head echoed. Phoenix opened the large plate-glass door that led to the patio of his hillside house and sought a direction.

The voice was female.

She was in trouble.

She was mortal.

No, he revised immediately. Not mortal. The strength in her mental cry meant something else ran through her veins, something that gave her the ability to call to an Elemental, even inadvertently.

"Nice dog. Handsome dog. Pack. A pack. Run! Run!"

He plucked the impression of very large dogs from her brain. He paused, revising his thoughts. Wolves. Werewolves.

Did this call for his intervention? It was not his concern.

The wings on his back did not appear idly. It was a lie that he wasn't involved.

Perhaps other paranormals would help her? He cast out mentally, searching for any sign that someone besides himself had heard her cry for help and was acting.

There were plenty of additional minds, but none seemed to be interested in her plight.

Typical. Most paranormals had a disregard for humans that bordered on disdain. Except she wasn't human. He recognized that she thought she was; perhaps that was why nobody appeared to be going to her aid. Whatever the reason, no help was imminent.

His task, then. Even if his wings hadn't appeared, he couldn't ignore the cry. Why, though? Why this mortal—or whatever she was—and why now?

Answers would have to wait. With a hop through the open door and a glide onto the wind, Phoenix was in the air. He soared upward, his red-and-orange wings unfurling fully when he found a good current. Focusing, he determined the source of the altercation was several miles from his current location. Oakland, east of San Francisco. Industrial. Dark. Perfect for an ambush.

The tableau started to coalesce as he got closer. Faint yips met his ears, an aural indicator he was heading in the right direction.

"No, don't come closer. Fuck, dead end."

Her distress propelled him to speed up, engaging his wings to make the most of the current.

The lights got dimmer as he approached the destination fixed in his mind. There was little traffic in this dilapidated part of Oakland. Many of the streetlamps were out, so there were long stretches of darkness, broken only by ineffective pools of weak light.

A woman stood her ground in the corner of an alley sandwiched between two large warehouses. She was trapped between the high fence guarding the property behind and the beasts in front of her. Werewolves, Phoenix confirmed as he got closer. Untrained, young, stupid werewolves. Their black-tipped fur told him this was Fenley's clan. Running in a pack, the wolves clearly thought they were invulnerable to anything but other predators of the night. Just stupid wolves out for some fun, terrorizing the local population, toying with a human.

Silently landing behind the wolves, Phoenix folded his wings, and they slipped behind his back until they looked like another grouping of large muscles on his already massive frame.

The woman who had inadvertently sent out the distress call looked over. Only the widening and slight shift sideways of her eyes told him that she had seen him.

She *saw* him. She appeared odd, though, as if she was caught in a dream of some sort. There was something off about her mental signature, but he couldn't pinpoint it.

It made sense if she was other than human. In his Phoenix form he was shielded from their eyes, looking like an ordinary man. His wings could not be seen by humans, only paranormals.

She coughed and shot him a look under the cover of her thick wave of honey-blonde hair, a motion unseen by the wolves. His warrior side approved. Whatever was going on, she seemed alert enough.

"Nice doggies."

It was a beautiful voice, with a low register and silky, rounded tones.

The wolves were growling, their teeth bared, slowly pacing in front of her, closing possible avenues of escape with their constant movement. Foam escaped from the teeth of the largest wolf, giving it a rabid look. Their heavy leg muscles bunched as they circled, a readiness to spring at any moment evident.

Phoenix's wing feathers brushed against the crumbling concrete wall he leaned against. The air smelled of grease and used tires. Old cigarette cartons, fast-food bags and other human garbage littered the ground. The wolves had a den in a park not too far from here, and this would be a logical area for them to rove in. But their lack of discipline in targeting a human surprised him. Stupid, to draw attention to themselves.

Glancing over, he registered that the woman was pretty, tall and solid, with an athletic build. Phoenix mentally calculated her bulk, considering how much her weight would affect his center of gravity.

The passionate side of him admired the blonde facing down three young wolves. She looked from one to the next, clearly trying not to show her fear. The shaking of her body and quivering lips told him that the effort failed, valiant though it was.

She continued to look at him, and her eyes were wide, as if appealing to him for help. She still had that odd overlay, almost as if she was sleepwalking while awake. When the woman shifted again, he acted.

"Children, children," he chastised them, getting closer to the wolves while still keeping enough distance for a quick getaway. Caught as they were between two buildings, it would be difficult to grab her and take off, the retreat a sharp trajectory up and out.

A fireball might help. With a flick of mental energy, it was there. Flame danced lightly over his skin and collected at his fingertips.

All three wolves whirled, haunches quivering as they assessed Phoenix's unexpected presence. Their eyes flicked to the fireball and then, strangely, to the woman.

The largest of the three moved toward him, making a low series of yips.

The yips translated as a demand for him to back off. Now.

Phoenix shook his head. They obviously knew who Phoenix was, as they should. All the paranormals were aware of the Elementals. When he arrived seven years ago, he had introduced himself to the locals, so the packs knew that he was currently in San Francisco. They also had learned he didn't concern himself with other paranormal business. He left them alone to conduct their affairs and asked that they do the same.

The one who looked the fastest also yipped, and he translated the feral voice in his mind easily, as if the wolf were speaking the English language.

"Whatcha want, Elemental? Can't you see we're dealing with business? Clear out. Leave us alone. This doesn't concern you."

Phoenix turned his attention to the wolf mind-speaking to him.

"The better to rend you with, my dear," the wolf said, his mental tone mocking.

Did humans know a werewolf had been the inspiration for the Big Bad Wolf?

"Mortals are off-limits," Phoenix replied in the yip of wolf language. His hands had tensed into fists, his wings silently spreading over his back under the cloak of darkness, but not yet ready for flight. *"Go play with something that can defend itself."*

The bigger one stepped forward with a swagger. Phoenix could see the ripple under his skin. It wouldn't take much for the wolf to attack. They were angry and they were…scared? The quivering of their haunches told him they weren't as fearless as they appeared. One of them had marks across his back, as if he had been singed. Phoenix sniffed the air, but the overlay of scents made it impossible to pick up anything else.

He focused on the woman again. There was something else there, something flickering beneath her surface. It called to him, spoke to him in a way he hadn't felt for centuries. Fire. He shook his head, and he tasted the air again. There was fear and…something else. Compulsion, perhaps, as if their minds weren't quite under their own control.

It stank of Haures. His Demonos counterpart had a hand in this.

The largest wolf gestured to the blonde, but Phoenix didn't follow his hand. The distraction technique was too obvious. The third one moved into a classic flanking pattern until they had him triangulated.

The woman shifted now, opening her mouth as she observed the last wolf fall into place. She had blanched when the wolves surrounded them but managed to keep her cool. Amazingly, she still had her handbag, which she had slung crosswise on her body.

"Sir, you, the d-d-dogs…" she started and ground to a stop.

Time for fire. He gathered the flames at his fingertips and, with what appeared to be a casual flick, sent them toward the wolves. Fire stroked their ruffs, singeing the black tips. They yelped but didn't stand down. The aroma of burned fur slid across his nostrils and was quickly gone.

The wolves were shaking, he confirmed, by turns frightened and hostile, their foaming jaws and quivering haunches indicating a desire to rend, destroy, ruin. They hadn't yet moved on him, just positioned themselves to attack. They were scared. Of fire. Of him. Of her.

Her. But why? Even though she was some sort of half-breed, she seemed harmless. Still, there was something about her that frightened the wolves. Delving into her mind revealed that it was clouded, but there was a ring of fire. Interesting.

"What's your name?"

"Rachel."

She glanced at the triangulated wolves again.

She did not appear to be hurt; he didn't see blood or torn skin or anything other than mussed clothes from being snapped at.

The wolves would live to see another day.

"Good."

Phoenix pushed on her mentally, and her unconscious body slumped to the ground.

With a swift movement, Phoenix unfurled his wings and simultaneously rushed past the middle wolf to grab the woman and haul her into his arms. Her weight unbalanced him, making him lower to the ground. He concentrated for a second, recalibrating his center of gravity. Then, with strong flaps of his wings, he soared upward and flew out of reach of the snarling, snapping wolves in two strokes. They jumped, leaping with strong movements of their hind legs, trying fruitlessly to catch him. The yips of frustration and fury faded as they continued into the sky.

He was Phoenix. He could destroy three werewolf cubs with one heated burst of flame, but that would antagonize the locals. Better this way.

It was clear the woman's predicament had been the reason his wings had appeared. There was no other possibility he could sense, on the air or in his mind. It could only have been the shapeshifters and the scared woman.

The curses of the cubs faded in the distance as he flew, hampered by the woman in his arms. They thought they had been clever, but their efforts had been useless against a being that could fly. Recognizing him, they should have known that.

Then there was the problem of the woman. Her skin was soft and warm under his touch, and felt pliable. She couldn't be more than twenty-five. He looped her arms around his neck to keep her body stable, and the press of her left breast against his chest made his pulse increase and his body react. The muscles of her thighs over his forearms were taut and strong. She was big, but not overweight, a tall and well-built woman with solid warmth.

Phoenix continued his flight, soaring above unlighted or ill-lighted streets to get them close to the address he had plucked out of her mind. While he couldn't be seen, he wasn't sure about his passenger. There was a drumbeat of danger somewhere, and he wanted to get her home quickly.

The danger tugged at him. Challenge was coming, of that he was certain. Was this woman somehow intertwined with it? That would be new.

They reached the apartment building. Phoenix landed in the deserted street. He found the keys in her purse and sorted through them in his mind until the right one became clear. Just one lock, he noticed. Not secure at all.

It was a small one-bedroom, sparsely furnished and uninteresting. The only interesting thing was the intriguing woman who still lay unconscious in his arms.

Phoenix kicked the door shut behind them and strode to the open door of the bedroom. As in the living room, the furnishings were simple, clean but not expensive, and slightly used.

It was, at best, a middle-class lifestyle, he observed before settling her on the solid dark-blue comforter and laying her head on the matching blue-covered pillow.

There was a hiss and he turned to see a brown tabby cat growling at him, its ears flat.

His track record of cats disliking him stayed perfect, judging from the ears and the hissing. Tipping a wing at her small champion, Phoenix removed her shoes. Then he worked the comforter out from under her prone body and smoothed it over Rachel's form until it was up around her shoulders.

"Watch over her, kitty," he said, resisting an urge to press a kiss to her forehead. Something inside her called to him, something as integral to him as the fire he utilized. The cat continued to glare at him, its green eyes glinting in the semidarkness as he checked and locked the front door.

Either the door or a window would have to stay unlocked if he left without waking her. Choosing a bedroom window that faced a brick building next door, he gave the cat, and then Rachel, a final look. With a strange reluctance to leave the woman echoing through his body, Phoenix exited.

The green of the cat's disdainful eyes was the last thing he saw as he closed the window. The cat jumped on the bed as he watched. Phoenix hovered for another second, watching Rachel stir before he turned and soared upwards.

It would have been better to ignore her distress call. It was not his business. Even with Challenge upon him, he should have let it be. But he could not. If Haures had been involved, the reason was unclear. The woman's origin was also opaque, his sense that she had fire still dancing in his mind. It was a mystery, and he did not like those. Especially when it was time for Challenge.

He took to the air. His intention was to go above the clouds and float there, unseen, observing the Earth. It never failed to soothe him.

Except, perhaps, for tonight.

❧ ❧

Rachel woke with a jerk, sweat beading her forehead and covering her body. Her hands clutched the covers. For a moment she thought someone was in the room with her, and she cried out before stopping herself.

Oh no. It happened again.

She glanced around wildly, letting the atmosphere seep into her mind. She heard little other than the ambient noise of late evening or early morning—she wasn't sure which. She focused. Birds, large birds, soaring and flying, darting in and out of her path until they became a tangle of wings and feathers. They appeared almost human as they dove, knotting her hair with their huge orange-and-red feathers. Wolves howled, their canines bared, trotting menacingly back and forth, morphing into humans and then back to wolves again. Rachel shook her head. The dreams, so real, whirred in her mind until she finally allowed herself to relax, seeing only the familiar lines of her apartment.

She found the nightstand light and turned it on. The halogen lit the small bedroom, flooding her with welcome illumination. It had happened again. Damn it, it had happened again.

Were there any fires? Any scorch marks?

Her cat, JT, was at the foot of the bed, his posture watchful, intent. When she focused on him, he started licking the fur on his ruff as if that was what he had been doing the entire time.

The last thing she remembered was… She concentrated, the details slow to focus in her mind. She recalled nothing after getting on the subway, and had no idea of where she had gone. She didn't remember coming home or going to bed. She didn't remember anything after she'd gotten on BART. Rachel peered at the clock, the LED numbers telling her it was twelve fifty-three. Damn it. She had lost several hours. Again. Luckily, she was home, and unhurt.

Rachel eased herself from the bed. Had those been the clothes she'd gone to work in? She thought for a moment and decided that they were. No shoes, though. She flexed her limbs one at a time, checking for soreness. She sniffed the air, tense with anticipation. Smelling nothing but night and a faint stench of her own sweat, Rachel let out a breath.

The dreams struck her again, and she staggered. Large birds, more human than bird; vivid dreams of a half man, half bird swooping down to rescue her from dogs? In the dream they felt like wolves. Wolves in Oakland? That made as much sense as bird/human hybrids did, she thought ruefully. That was how dreams worked. Fire was another component of her dreams, and not always confined to her subconscious.

Odd dreams had been part of her psyche since she was ten years old. If she'd had these types of dreams before then, she didn't remember then. Like most other things from her first ten years, they were a blur, the memories impossible to reach except in snippets.

Winged men. Wolves shifting. The dreams circled her vision, playing over and over again in her mind. Rachel cursed, and JT gave her a look of feline disdain.

No question her fugue states were getting worse. She focused, trying to remember something, anything, from her time on BART. All she could remember was wolves and men and the feeling that she had been saved by something she didn't understand.

She prayed that nothing had happened at work, but she couldn't be sure. One more blackout at the office, one more unexplained and unexplainable fire, and she was done for. Rachel wondered if that would be for the best.

JT jumped off the bed to stand in front of the window in the far corner of her bedroom. He meowed, then again, and a third time. It was a persistent, shrill meow, unlike his usual laconic sound. He continued until she finally rose and went to the window.

It was unlocked. She shook her head. Even in a second-floor apartment, Rachel made sure to keep all access points locked. It had been a habit of hers since before she could remember most things. She didn't recall why.

A ripple went through her body, goose bumps rising on her skin, making all the hairs stand on end. With a flick of her wrist, she locked the window again, testing the pane to ensure that it was truly sealed.

Satisfied, JT began licking his paw and then rolled over in front of her feet, presenting his back to her. Rachel reached down and scratched the brown-striped fur until he purred.

She'd been poked and prodded, and nobody had found anything wrong, but the fugue states continued. She'd seen a therapist who seemed more interested in her family life than the blackouts. When they happened, she would be unaware of her surroundings for anywhere from under a minute to several hours, like last night. She didn't normally associate the blackouts with flying man/birds, however. That was new. They were usually accompanied by something burning. Last night had been new in a variety of ways.

Her mail lay strewn across the large, round oak table by the door. It had been neglected the past few days. Maybe the task of sorting mail would soothe her. Unfortunately, the piles of paper did nothing to ease the images in her head. *Birds. Wolves. Fire. Fire. Fire.*

JT meowed again, and this time she picked him up, his soft fur tickling her cheek. She scratched the cat behind the ears, luxuriating in his loud purr.

"What do you think, JT?" She wasn't too fond of slobbery dogs, and cats were easier for apartment life.

Dogs. *Dogs.* Wolves. A sliver of the dream or her fugue state came back to her. When the first dog-wolf came trotting up, it had turned and snarled at her. Then the second one joined it and the third, all growling.

Rachel knew you were supposed to stand your ground in front of dogs and not show fear. She had a vague recollection, or perhaps it was a dream, that when they surrounded her, she had reacted by flinging her hands, and something had discharged from them. She thought she had smelled smoke. Then they had charged, their teeth bared, and she had run. They had loped after her, keeping three paces behind but not letting her out of their sight. Yelling for help had yielded nothing but the sound of her voice bouncing off the buildings in the deserted industrial area.

An image of the flying man came to her, in that foggy quality that dreams had. With her life in danger, she shouldn't have noticed him, but she had. Even with wolves barking around her, she'd seen that he was handsome in a craggy way, with short brown hair and a heavily muscled but sleek body, tall and fit. He called to the deeply feminine part of her that had been too often neglected.

Rachel shuddered. The door was locked and chained, but the window had been open. A flying man could have gone out that way. The drop to the ground would have been no obstruction to someone with wings. She almost felt the sensation of the wind on her face, and for a moment it seemed as if she had, at one point in her life, flown without a craft.

She shook herself, sending mail scattering across the table. Flying people didn't exist and neither did werewolves. It was a weird, bizarre, unexplainable *dream*. Either that or she was going crazy.

Sensing a tingle, she checked her palms. Had she been clenching her hands too tightly? Her palms were red in that blistered way of sunburns. There was an odd smell in the air, as if someone had struck matches and let them burn all the way down. She rubbed suddenly itchy hands together and stared at the mail.

Rachel wiped at a char mark on the table. It hadn't been there a week ago, but she had woken up from one of her fugue states to find it etched into the table and a piece of junk mail smoldering on the floor. She had put it out, the acrid smell of the coated paper as well as her fear searing her. It was similar to events she'd had in the office and, once, in her car.

What in the hell was happening?

The first ripple of the earthquake was so slight that Rachel would have slept through it under normal circumstances. Quakes were a fact of life in San Francisco, and small ones happened all the time. If you panicked over each one, you wouldn't last long.

JT flicked his ears at the slight ground movement but seemed as unconcerned as his owner. Rachel continued to sort through bills, noting that her shades swayed a little. She picked up the junk mail to toss into the recycling, and began to move to the kitchen area.

A loud rumble alerted her that she only had seconds to act. Dropping the junk mail to the floor, Rachel leaped for JT and scooped him into her arms before he could run.

A big earthquake was coming. A bad one too, if the rumble was any indication. Her building was relatively new and up to code, but there was never a way to tell for sure if a building would survive the big one.

She dumped the now-squirming cat into the soft-sided top-loading carrier that always stood open in the corner and zipped it up. If claws and teeth were any indication, escape was the only thing on JT's mind.

The quake struck, and she tossed JT onto the queen-size bed, joining him there. She'd taken some earthquake safety courses when she moved out to San Francisco, and one of the things they said was that the bed was one of the safest places to be. It was better than a slamming door in a doorway or under flimsy furniture. It was better than outside, with falling glass and exposed, live electrical wires.

The headboard slammed into the wall, and the shades and ceiling lights swayed. The room moved—*bam bam bam*—a hard jolt shaking the walls. Rachel clung to the carrier, JT yowling loudly, while holding on to the side of the bed with her free hand. Her body warmed, just as her hands had earlier. It wasn't the first time over the past few weeks that heat had flushed through her body. If she hadn't been twenty-five, she might have thought she was going into menopause. It felt as if bees were just under her skin, buzzing to get out.

Rachel visually measured the distance between the bed and the door in case the walls started to buckle. The lights flickered but didn't go out. Her skin felt loose and heavy, as if it were sloughing off her body. A quick glance outside showed that the outside lights were fine and…

Strangely, the streetlights weren't swaying or flickering. Beyond the frantic beat of her heart, there were no sounds. Car alarms should be going *woop woop* by now in shrieking disharmony, triggered by the motion of the rolling earth.

The hissing of her feline drew Rachel's attention back to the room, and she clicked her tongue in reassurance to JT, but her gaze lingered on the outside tableau. The room was still rolling and jerking. Rachel thought she saw…

Eyes.

There were eyes outside.

Red, glowing, very unfriendly eyes. Floating outside her window.

Rachel shrieked internally but showed no outward fear. Her skin burned, and she wanted to… What did she want to do? She wasn't sure.

❧ ☙

Even if Phoenix had been sleeping, the shrill mental scream would have pierced his consciousness. He caught a glimpse of rolling furniture and red eyes, and cursed. Not his image, not his mind. The woman. The—whatever she was. Rachel.

First the wolves and now the shadow people? The paranormal had a hard-on for this woman.

No time for a shirt. His shirts were well crafted, but even the best stitching got in the way in desperate times. Sweats and feathers would have to do.

A peek into the woman's mind confirmed his suspicion. It could have been vampires, they had those red eyes—a trick of the light and the fluids that kept their biology going. But he was betting on the shadow people. He sent a quick mental blast to her, praying it would be enough until he got there.

"Hold on," he said into her mind, hoping she was strong enough to accept his mental signal. *"I am coming."*

What he got back was a sense of fear but also of heat, like she was ready to go up in flames. He hurried to the door.

❧ ❧

"I am coming."

As the room rolled, Rachel glanced outside several times and confirmed that nothing else was behaving the same way. This event was confined to her apartment.

The dream last night.

Red eyes and then dark mist, shadowy forms and a hiss.

"Open the door."

"They" wanted her outside.

The dream last night. It hadn't been a dream.

With that acceptance, for the first time since her fugue states started, the memory flooded back. The strange dogs/wolves, the winged man, the flight home. Although she had been unconscious, part of her mind had been linked to his, and she wasn't sure if she was remembering or seeing through his eyes. There was the feeling of flight, the sensation of feathers on the wing and air currents passing them like strong wind in a storm, vivid in her mind.

Birds? Wolves? Red eyes outside? *This is crazy.*

"Open the door. Open the window. Let us in."

The room still rolled, and even JT had started to settle down, as the rumble showed no signs of abating.

"I am coming. Don't go outside." It was the man's voice, urgent, rushed and closer.

Was this earthquake real? Or was it in her mind? JT was feeling it, so it was somehow physically manifesting, but how? Her skin continued to heat and her forearms developed red streaks. Something deep within her stirred, an animal clawing to get out.

"Don't open the door. Don't open the window. Don't go outside. I am almost there." In the madness, the familiarity of the man's voice reassured her.

"Open the door. Open the window. Let us in." Rachel struggled between the two, trying to focus on the former and ignore the latter.

Rachel hung JT's carrier around her shoulder and then clutched her hands to her ears, as if that could keep the voices out. She wanted to run, wanted to yank open the door and go outside, obeying the commands of the red eyes. It would be so much easier that way.

Vampires needed to be invited in, didn't they?

Vampires? Really?

She heard a whoosh and a rustle as if wings were settling. The birdman...she groped for the name, found it...Phoenix. She had no idea how she knew his name, but it was Phoenix.

"Shadow people. Not vampires. I am here."

The voice inside her mind was different from the shadow people's voices. Rachel's body flooded with relief.

As if on cue, the room stopped shaking. The heat in her body began to subside. She still felt its lingering presence and saw the air around her shimmer as if a fire had burned in front of her.

"Get some things. You can't stay here."

Keeping JT slung over her shoulder, she grabbed her purse and a toiletry bag she always kept packed, tossed them into a handy tote, and went for the door. JT yowled, moving from side to side in the carrier.

Flinging the door open, Rachel gaped at the naked torso of the well-built man standing on her exterior landing. He seemed agitated, harried, his wing feathers askew. She squeaked but made no other sound when red eyes appeared behind him, several feet away but out of reach of his wingspan.

He followed her gaze and growled. The beings pulled back but still remained visible.

"Good thing you didn't let them in."

There was a hiss behind him. *"Let us have the human."*

"Not a chance." There was steel in Phoenix's tone, something she wouldn't have thought was possible when speaking telepathically.

"Come on, Rachel. We have to go. It's not safe."

The world was turning upside down in a big hurry, but staying there meant death. The shadow people, or vampires or whatever they were would find a way in sooner or later. The wolves would get her. Something. Something would get her.

Why?

"JT comes."

His brows lowered, brown slashes against his forehead. "He's your responsibility. We have to fly. Now. Are you ready?"

Rachel gestured to the tote. "I always have a bag packed."

"Just walk away." One of the red-eyed beings poked a finger at Phoenix, but its eyes were on Rachel.

He motioned to her as if there hadn't been a mental voice. Rachel decided that it hadn't been meant for her to hear.

"Let's go," Phoenix said, his voice urgent.

She put her arms around him. Phoenix frowned at the touch of her body.

"You're hot," he said, his voice a growl.

"I know," she said and that was all there was time for. With a swift motion, they were up and in the air. Behind them slight, wispy figures lingered by the apartment, their eyes glowing in the night.

Phoenix and Rachel were flying near the clouds before he spoke again.

"Why do they want you so badly?"

About the Author

Claire has written on and off for most of her life, starting with fan fiction when she was very young. She writes across a wide range of genres, and does not consider any of it off limits or out of reach. If a story calls to her, she will write it. She currently lives in Los Angeles and spends her free time writing novels and short stories, as well as doing animal rescue and enjoying the sunshine. Claire's website is www.clairedavon.com.

Interested in learning more about Claire and her stories? Signing up for her newsletter is easy! Just go to: https://clairedavon.com/newsletter/ and you will have access to news, as well as giveaways and special bonus content only available to her subscribers!

ELEMENTALS' CHALLENGE

Fire Danger

Air Attack

Water Fall

SHIFTER WARS

No Ordinary Fairy

UNIVERSE CHRONICLES

Shifting Auras

www.ingramcontent.com/pod-product-compliance
Lightning Source LLC
Chambersburg PA
CBHW070505170726
48291CB00008B/2667

9781946621092